"Clearly pictures the ingenuity needed for survival in the wilderness. A modern Robinson Crusoe whose exploits reward the reader with a vivid picture of genuine heroism." —*The Christian Science Monitor*

"An exciting book." —San Francisco *Chronicle*

"[Readers] will be impressed by Steve's courage." —ALA *The Booklist*

Pilot Down, Presumed Dead

by MARJORIE PHLEGER

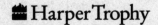

HarperTrophy

A Division of HarperCollins*Publishers*

ACKNOWLEDGMENT

Technical advice furnished by Captain Francisco Muñoz of Servicio Aereo Baja and by Fred B Phleger of Scripps Institution of Oceanography is gratefully acknowledged.

Pilot Down, Presumed Dead

Chapter 1

THE BRIGHT BLUE OF THE AUGUST SKY WAS RELIEVED by occasional puffs of white clouds as Steve Ferris climbed into his single-engine plane to fly back to the United States. The runway at La Paz airport, near the tip of Mexico's Baja California peninsula, reflected the brilliance of the noonday sun.

His three passengers delivered safely, Steve prepared to make the long flight back to San Diego, where he was co-owner of a small but flourishing flying school. It was a round-trip flight he had made several times in the past two years owing to the popularity of deep-sea fishing in the Gulf of California. He or his partner, Ben Phillips, occasionally took time off to fly charter groups to the few settlements along the Gulf Coast that had boats and tackle available for the sport.

The charter trips were a profitable sideline for the youthful partners. The eight-hundred-mile peninsula stretching south of the U.S.–Mexican border near San Diego was still for the most part an undeveloped wilderness of deserts, canyons, high barren mountains, and long lonely beaches. The few dirt roads were often impassable, and settlements were scarce and widely separated. Tourists with limited time and no wish to brave the hazards of land travel were eager to charter private planes to take them to the excellent fishing in the Gulf.

Usually when he had a charter trip as far south as La Paz, Steve spent the night in the Mexican town, which was more than seven hundred miles from San Diego. Today, however, he had planned to complete the round trip. The return trip would take a little over five hours, including his check-in at the border town of Tijuana and at Lindbergh Field in San Diego.

When he had filed his flight plan at the La Paz tower, he had made his usual inquiry about expected weather conditions. As far as the Mexican officials were informed, the conditions were favorable for flying: good visibility and no rain. Weather information in sparsely settled Baja was naturally limited. There was no telephone service except near the U.S. border, and communication was by ham radio and a limited number of radio telephones.

Waving *adios* to the two Mexicans who had filled his gas tanks, Steve fastened his seat belt and started his engine. Permission for the take-off was granted from the tower, and he taxied to the end of the

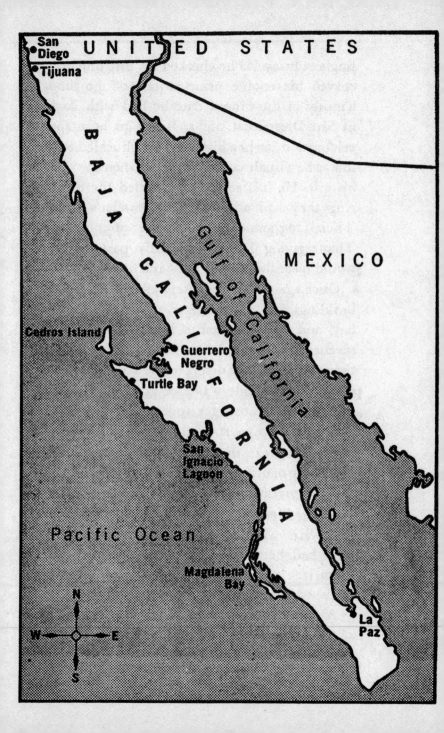

single runway. As he checked his instruments and revved his engine prior to take-off he thought happily of the dinner date he had with Barbara in San Diego that night. It was to be a special celebration for her birthday. He chuckled to himself as he visualized her surprise when she opened his gift. He had secretly purchased the diamond ring they had admired in a jeweler's window. Their engagement was to be announced on Thanksgiving Day at a family party, and she would have the ring to show relatives and friends.

Once again airborne, Steve circled over the low buildings and palm-fringed esplanade along the bay and headed west. Climbing gradually to seventy-five hundred feet, he settled back to cross the great stretch of desert to the Pacific Coast. On the seat at his side a box of crackers, two candy bars, and some oranges and bananas hastily purchased at the airport would do for lunch when he felt hungry. On the floor of the cockpit was the gallon jug of drinking water that he always carried. It was a precautionary measure in case of a forced landing. Most of the Baja peninsula was desert, and water was very scarce or nonexistent. Pilots who had been forced down had often suffered from lack of water and in a few cases had even perished from thirst before they were found.

After an hour of flying, Steve glimpsed the blue of the Pacific Ocean ahead. In a few more minutes

12

he was over Magdalena Bay and turning the Cessna north to fly along the coast. Glancing down, he noted that the ocean was dotted with white caps. They appeared to be increasing in size even as he looked.

"That's odd," he said to himself. "The ocean was as calm as a millpond on the way down this morning."

Through the vents he could hear the wind whistling at a more than normal rate. Far out on the horizon, clouds seemed to be building up into huge thunderheads. Steve was not unduly alarmed; he had seen this happen before when he was flying. It usually indicated a far-off storm.

As he winged onward toward San Ignacio Lagoon he kept his eye on the clouds. They were turning darker and seemed to be racing toward the barren coast. For the first time a feeling of apprehension crept into Steve's mind. He had often been caught in rainstorms while flying, so he had no fear of an ordinary downpour. These clouds, however, had an ominous look about them.

He reached for his air map. On it he had marked a few abandoned dirt landing strips that were scattered along his route. As he feared, there were no marked strips within the immediate vicinity. He noted that the nearest sizable settlement was the town of Guerrero Negro, one hundred miles to the north. He calculated the length of time it

13

would take to reach the town. Bucking the strong gusts of wind would slow him down, and he could not possibly make it in less than forty-five minutes. He knew that the storm would be upon him before that.

Steve grabbed his earphones and turned on his small radio. He was too far from La Paz, but it might be possible to make contact with the settlement at Turtle Bay or with some ham radio operator on a nearby ranch. In case he was forced to land someplace in the vast uninhabited area, he knew it was essential to report his position if he was to be rescued. He called his signal over and over, but there was no response.

Suddenly the storm hit the plane in all of its fury. Rain pelted the fuselage, and an abnormally strong gale caught the wings in its grip. Steve struggled with the controls in an effort to keep the light plane upright. Meanwhile he continued to call his signal repeatedly, adding "Mayday, Mayday," the call of distress. Finally he had to give up the radio and concentrate on fighting the storm, which had suddenly increased to hurricane force. He buckled on his shoulder harness and tightened his seat belt as the black clouds closed around him, turning day into night. The plane bounced up and down and shook and shivered as the gale threatened to tear the frail wings from the fuselage.

14

Steve now realized that he was caught in a dreaded *chubasco*, the name the Mexicans had given to sudden summer tropical storms of hurricane intensity. He had heard tales of the damage caused by these unpredictable storms. Ships at sea had been blown off course, and some had suffered serious damage to booms or sails.

Enveloped in the black mass of clouds and pelting rain which was hitting the plane horizontally, he could hear the unearthly roar of the wind. He peered below, but there was nothing to see, as land and ocean were completely obscured. As he fought to keep the craft steady he had the feeling that he was being blown miles out to sea.

The altimeter needle was now dropping at a fast rate: 3,000! 2,900! 2,800! The needle continued its downward sweep, erasing feet by the second. At 1,000 feet it seemed to steady, but a cold sweat broke out on Steve's forehead as he realized that the choppy sea was probably directly below him. A particularly gusty downdraft could send the plane plunging down into the black waves. If he were forced into the sea, Steve knew that it would mean certain death. The Cessna would sink almost immediately. Even if he were able to extricate himself in time, he knew that it would be impossible to swim against the turbulence of the storm-tossed waves.

He kept his eye on the altimeter as he worked the controls. Now the needle was moving dangerously downward again. Steve prayed silently as it registered lower and lower. He knew that he was completely helpless against the mighty force of the gale.

After a nightmare quarter of an hour, the violent bucking of the plane seemed to lessen. The altimeter needle now registered 300 feet and no longer wavered. The atmosphere had turned from inky black to a dirty gray, and the wild shrieking of the gale through the vents seemed to be abating.

Encouraged by these signs of a possible lull in the storm, Steve pulled back on the stick as hard as he could in a frantic attempt to gain altitude. As he peered through the rain-streaked window he suddenly tensed.

Looming ahead he caught a glimpse of land through the swirling clouds. In a few seconds the gray curtain closed, and he was again in the murky void. Steve's first thought at the brief sight of land was that he had been blown in a circle and was back over the coast again. If this was true, it was an answer to his prayer.

"But that doesn't seem possible," he muttered to himself. "I must have been right over the coast the whole time."

16   He noted with relief that the plane was now at an altitude of 650 feet. He made an immediate decision. He must try for a landing in case the

storm renewed its fury. To make any kind of a landing except a suicidal crash, he knew that he would require a long and level piece of ground. It should be a clear stretch of one thousand feet.

Keeping his eyes fixed on the window, he prayed for another break in the clouds. As if in answer to his prayer, the gray curtain parted again. Dead ahead he saw a long sandy beach with towering waves breaking on the shore. This was it! He had to try it.

As the plane approached the beach the clouds miraculously rolled away, as if pushed by an unseen hand. Steve now had a clear view of the terrain that bounded the beach. It was ridged with low, bush-covered sand dunes, stretching as far as he could see. At either end of the beach were rocks and cliffs. He knew that he would have to land on the beach itself. He had never attempted a beach landing before, but now he had no choice. He would have to get down immediately or take a chance again in the renewed force of the gale. If the beach was long enough and the wet sand moderately firm, he could land with a margin of safety.

There was no time to make a cautious circle to observe the beach or to try out the sand with his wheels before landing. The storm was building up again, and he had to get down or risk being blown out to sea.

As he tensed for the landing Steve noted that

one thing was in his favor. The tide was low enough so that he had plenty of room on the wet sand to keep the plane away from the surf.

Lower and lower the plane dropped, until at last it was skimming along above the sand. Finally, the wheels touched. Too late, Steve realized that the sand was soft! The wheels dug in with a series of jolts and bumps. Sand flew up in clouds. Suddenly, with a tremendous jerk, the light craft tilted over on the whirring propeller!

The last thing Steve was conscious of, as his fingers groped for the key and turned off the ignition, was a mighty crash on his head. Then he blacked out.

In a matter of minutes the storm had again gathered its forces. The sky closed in. Rain and sand beat on the fuselage unmercifully as it lay upside down with its inert form inside. The wind lashed furiously at the wings, but the bent propeller, deeply embedded in the sand, kept the craft anchored to the ground.

At last the storm blew itself out. The dark clouds receded seaward and dissipated. The waves settled down to their normal crests, but along the beach, as mute testimony to the violence of the gale, lay the dead bodies of sea birds and fish. Driftwood, seaweed, and other debris washed ashore by the waves littered the sand.

Chapter 2

||||||||||||||||||||||||||||||||||||||||||||||||||||||||||||||||||||||||||||||||

GRADUALLY STEVE OPENED HIS EYES. HIS HEAD throbbed, and he had difficulty in focusing. As full consciousness returned, he discovered that he was hanging from his shoulder harness, with his head resting on the ceiling of the cockpit. His harness and tight seat belt had saved him from crashing through the window as the plane flipped over.

After carefully extricating himself from the harness, he dropped on the ceiling and lay for a moment fighting the dizziness which resulted from hanging upside down. As soon as his head cleared, he felt all over his body for broken bones. He was relieved to find that he was unharmed except for a bump on his head as big as an egg.

Everything in the plane cabin that was movable lay on the ceiling in a jumbled mass. With difficulty Steve crawled to the door and managed to wrench it open. He let himself down carefully on the wet sand. Although his head ached and his body was stiff and sore, he pulled himself upright and proceeded to take stock of the situation.

He saw that the storm had subsided and that

19

it was still daylight. Lifting his wrist watch to his ear, he found that it was still running. The time was five minutes after four. He figured that he must have been unconscious for nearly two hours.

The late afternoon light, as an aftermath of the storm, was murky, but it was sufficient to enable Steve to examine the damage to the Cessna. He saw that the wheels in striking the soft sand had suddenly arrested the progress of the plane and caused it to tilt over on the propeller. With its momentum halted so abruptly, the craft had turned completely over. As a result, the propeller was bent, and the landing gear had collapsed. Two of the cabin windows were cracked, but not broken. The only other casualty that he found was the radio. He tried over and over to get some response, but even after restringing the antenna, which had come loose in the accident, he had to give up. His knowledge of electronics was limited, and he had no idea how to repair the instrument.

As he reconstructed the landing in his mind he was thankful that he had had sense enough to turn off the engine. Otherwise the gas might have ignited, and the plane and he would now be a smoldering heap of wreckage.

He made several futile attempts to turn the plane over, but it was impossible to do alone. The bent propeller, in any event, would keep him confined to the ground, even if he were able to right the plane and repair the landing gear. The only thing he could do was to stay on the beach and await rescue from the Mexicans or the U.S. Coast Guard. With night approaching, it was unlikely that anyone would search for him until the next day.

As he thought over the situation, Steve realized that he would not even be missed until he failed to report at the Tijuana airport around 6 P.M. If it was assumed that he had flown over the border without reporting in Tijuana, he would not be reported missing at Lindbergh Field in San Diego unless he failed to show up that night. It would take time to organize a rescue flight and several hours to fly to the area, so the earliest he could expect the Coast Guard or the Mexicans to pick him up would be the next afternoon.

The major complication, he realized, would be to locate him. He had no idea where he was. With his radio out of commission, he had no way of letting anyone know that he had crashed or when it had happened. All the information available to the search party was that he had left La Paz at noon and was probably on the ground somewhere along his route to Tijuana.

After exploring the beach and the dunes for a few hundred yards, Steve was convinced that he must have landed on one of the pocket beaches along the uninhabited coast between Turtle Bay and San Ignacio Lagoon. There were several of these indented little sandy stretches along the rugged coast, and he could be on any one of them. He knew that it would be unwise to attempt to walk in the dark to the nearest habitation, which could only be a remote ranch or fishing camp. It was better to stay by the plane, which could be easily spotted from the air.

Although his head still throbbed, Steve set to work to dig the Cessna's nose from the deep wet sand. He used a small shovel that he always carried in the cabin. As he worked, he thought of Barbara's disappointment when he did not appear for their date. She would call his apartment and getting no answer would assume that he had stayed the night in La Paz. The next day she would learn that he was reported missing. It was too bad she had to worry, but there was nothing to do but await rescue.

When he had exposed the bent propeller, Steve examined it carefully. As he had thought, it was beyond repair. A new prop would have to be flown down from San Diego before the Cessna could ever take to the air again.

When he crawled back into the cabin, he found his belongings mixed together helter-skelter. Water bottle, jacket, maps, oranges, bananas, crackers, candy bars, clipboard, and his sunglasses were piled in a heap. The water bottle, Steve noted with relief, was still whole and stoppered, and the fruit and crackers still edible. For the first time, he allowed himself to think of the necessity of food and water in case he had to be on the beach any length of time. He mentally calculated how long the gallon of water was likely to last. With strict rationing and no activity on his part, he figured that it would be sufficient for several days. For nourishment, the three oranges, three bananas, two candy bars, and the box of crackers would keep him for an equal length of time. Anyway, Steve assured himself, he would be found long before that.

His watch now read 6:30 P.M. The tide, which had been low when he landed, had risen in the meantime, and the water was a few feet from the plane. After examining the high-water mark, he concluded that the lower section of the beach, where the plane lay, would be flooded at high tide. However, there was no danger of the plane floating away; he estimated that the water depth could be only a couple of inches at its height.

As darkness descended on his lonely beach Steve settled himself in the cabin as comfortably as he could. The seats were still firmly attached upside down, and he had to stretch out on the ceiling with his rolled-up jacket as a cushion for his head. Although his hunger was acute, he allowed himself only a few crackers and one banana, which he washed down with several swallows of water. He was dead tired from his long day and the battle with the storm, but his mind was filled with plans to help in his rescue.

When it was daylight and low tide again, he decided that he would use the shovel to mark out a message in the wet sand. An enormous S O S should attract attention from the air. He would fill the depressed letters with white shells, which he had observed were plentiful on the dry sand of the upper beach. The white shells would make the letters much more visible. He also decided that if he was not found the next day he would gather driftwood for a huge fire. There was plenty of gas in the Cessna's tanks, and luckily he had a box of matches. A blazing fire at night might attract a passing shrimp boat or a turtle fisherman. After these decisions, Steve finally dropped off into an exhausted sleep.

Sometime in the middle of the night, he was awakened abruptly. Not knowing what had roused him, he stretched his cramped limbs and listened intently. Then he heard it. A weird howling noise repeated over and over.

Steve's flesh crawled as he rose and peered out of the plane window. All was pitch dark, but as he kept trying to adjust his eyes to the blackness the moon came out from behind some clouds and illuminated the beach.

A large coyote was standing on a sand dune about fifty yards from the plane. It was baying at the moon.

"Well, I'm not alone anyway," Steve observed to himself. "But I'd just as soon not get mixed up with that big fellow."

He opened the plane door to look at the surf, which was now lapping around the fuselage. At the noise the coyote bounded away.

Watching its hasty retreat, Steve thought: "He must be as scared of me as I am of him." He assumed that the animal had come down to the beach to feast on the dead birds and fish.

After reassuring himself that the plane was in no danger of floating away, Steve curled up and was soon sleeping soundly again.

Chapter 3

THE EARLY MORNING SUN SHINING IN THE PLANE windows waked Steve from a deep dream. In his dream he was sitting across the table from Barbara at Lubach's Restaurant in San Diego. In front of him was a rare steak, which he was just about to devour when he returned to reality. Opening his eyes, he came to with a start. The memory of the steak made his mouth water as he visualized its juicy tenderness. His stomach pangs reminded him that he had not had a square meal since an early breakfast the morning before.

Slowly raising himself from his cramped position in the cabin, Steve stretched his tired muscles and felt the bump on his head. The swelling had gone down some, but it was still sore to touch. His mouth and throat felt as dry as if he had swallowed a wad of cotton.

As he reached for his water bottle he told himself that he should take only a sip. The liquid, however, was so refreshing that he drank more than was wise. He knew that he should conserve the water, but he rationalized by reminding himself that he would be rescued this day or at the latest the next.

As he crawled out of the plane he noticed that the tide had receded. The plane was stuck in the wet sand, but fortunately the water had not leaked in during the night. The salt-water damage to the metal would be serious in time, but there was no way to avoid it.

Grabbing an orange to stay his hunger, he walked along the beach as he peeled and ate it. He chose a place in the wet sand to mark out the S O S. After he got his shovel, he debated whether it would be better to write HELP! or just stick to the conventional S O S. The latter, he decided, was preferable. It would mean more to a Mexican pilot than the English word.

Three quarters of an hour later he had completed the message, except for filling it in with shells. Each letter was about eight feet tall and half a foot deep in the sand. Using his jacket as a sack, he made many trips back and forth to the dry upper beach to get shells. With these he filled the depressed letters. When he had finished, the letters stood out clearly, and he was satisfied that they could easily be seen by a low-flying plane.

That job completed, Steve looked around for other means of attracting attention. Up on the dry sand, among the debris which had washed ashore in storms, he found a long narrow board.

After dragging it to the top of a nearby dune, he took off his white tee shirt and tied it to the end. He secured the other end deep in the sand, and when he had finished, his shirt flapped merrily in the morning breeze.

His next task was to locate and mark off a runway for a rescue plane. He tramped the whole length of the beach, which he estimated to be about a half-mile long. Although the beach curved at either end, the middle section was straight enough for a safe landing when the tide was low. He tested the wet sand for firmness before marking off the area. He wanted to be sure that the rescue plane would not flip over in soft sand as the Cessna had. Using his shovel, he marked a runway approximately eight hundred feet long. Until the tide rose again, the runway would guide any small plane to a landing.

When he had finished, the sun was high overhead and Steve's watch showed that it was noon. Although he had kept his ears alert and had glanced skyward every few minutes, he had neither heard nor seen any sign of an aircraft. The only noise on the beach was the cry of the sea birds and the background roar of the waves. The sky, washed clean by yesterday's storm, was a wide expanse of cloudless blue. The only moving things were flocks of gulls and pelicans.

Hunger pangs kept reminding him of his predicament. As he munched a few crackers and swallowed some water, he began to dwell on the potential seriousness of his situation. He was already weak from hunger and thirst, and the morning's work had further depleted his strength. It could take days for the searching party to locate him. The peninsula was too big and sparsely settled for his whereabouts to be easily pinpointed. His flight plan would give both the Mexicans and the U.S. Coast Guard something to go by, but they might assume that the storm had blown him off course. And worse yet, if they did not locate him within a reasonable length of time, they could assume that he had crashed in the ocean and was lost without a trace.

Hastily putting aside these gloomy thoughts, Steve stripped off his clothes and plunged into the surf. The cool water refreshed his dehydrated body and he felt much better.

As he emerged from his dip, he stopped to watch small schools of tiny fish darting around his feet in the shallow water. They seemed to be trying to escape larger fish in the deeper water. Out beyond the breakers curved black fins rising and falling indicated the presence of a group of porpoises that were feeding on the larger fish. Sea birds were diving into the waves to snatch a meal. Observing this abundance of fish and birds, Steve knew that he would not starve, no matter how long he had to wait for help.

29

"I will have to invent ways of catching them,"

he said to himself. "But I'll cross that bridge when it's necessary." He knew that drinking water would be his biggest worry if he were stranded on the beach for long.

When he had dressed, Steve again felt the bump on his head. The swelling had gone down, and his head was not as sore as it had been. The cool water had helped to reduce the inflammation. Although he felt considerably better, he was still hungry. Another few sips of water and a banana helped some. He measured the water left in the bottle. It was now down a quarter, which meant that he had about three quarts left. After an inventory of his food, he saw that he had two oranges, one banana, the candy bars, and half a box of crackers.

Thinking that he might be able to cook some of the dead fish and birds washed ashore by the storm, he examined a few, but he saw that they were already decomposing in the heat of the sun.

"Too bad for the coyote," Steve thought. "Last night was probably his first full meal in a long time." He had often wondered how the Baja California coyotes were able to keep from starving or from dying of thirst. There was so little water available.

It was now after two by Steve's watch. The tide had risen and would soon obliterate his marked runway and the S O S letters. If a plane appeared that afternoon it would not be able to land on the beach, but at least his position would be spotted, and he could be picked up the next day.

As the hands of his watch crept onward toward late afternoon Steve became more and more discouraged. He had hardly taken his eyes away from the sky for fear that he would miss seeing a plane, but the sky had remained empty. Two or three times he had started up, thinking that a distant high flying bird was a plane, but he soon learned not to be fooled.

To buoy up his sagging spirits, he set out to gather driftwood for a fire. "If I'm going to be here tonight, and it looks like I am," he decided, "I'll keep a fire burning up on the dry sand as long as I can stay awake."

As he collected wood for the fire Steve was amazed at the numerous items that he discovered up on the dry beach above the normal high-water mark. All sorts of things from ships had washed ashore in storms over the past years. Bottles, old life preservers, light bulbs, boxes, and crates littered the sand. From the sea there were whale and porpoise bones, sea lion skulls, net floats, and thousands of shells of different kinds and sizes. Deep in the sand were old bottles that had weathered to a deep purple or blue from many years on the sand and from exposure to the sun's rays. Medicine bottles, liquor bottles, cola containers, and many other glass receptacles had been thrown overboard by sailors on passing ships. Steve's mouth watered as he thought of the good things some of the bottles had contained.

In an hour he had piled enough wood on the dry beach to keep an enormous fire going for a long time.

Meanwhile the sun had dropped low in the sky, and he gave up all thoughts of being found that day. Forcing himself to stop scanning the sky, he kept doggedly adding wood to his reserve supply. His lack of nourishment was taking its toll. He found himself getting weaker and weaker as he expended energy collecting fuel. Soon he was so exhausted that he slumped down on the warm sand and dozed off.

Chapter 4

||||||||||||||||||||||||||||||||||||||||||||||||||||||||||||||||||||||||||||||

AS THE SUN SANK ON THE HORIZON STEVE WAKED
from his nap on the sand. He glanced at his watch
and saw that it was after six. Only an hour of daylight remained in which to prepare his fire and
make himself comfortable for the night.

His spirits were low as he contemplated another
night on the beach. It was cold and uncomfortable,
but it was nothing compared to what Barbara must
be experiencing. All the information she would
have was that he had disappeared from the air.
She would not know whether he was dead or alive.
He hoped that his parents in Chicago had not yet
been told of his disappearance.

Forcing himself to keep from dwelling on
thoughts of home, Steve got up and walked to the
plane. He found his box of matches and then drew
some gasoline from one of the tanks into a large
shell that he had picked up on the beach. He
carried it up on the dry sand to where he had
stacked the wood.

First he dug a shallow pit, then he placed
enough wood in it for a big fire. The wood was

33

still damp from the storm, but he sprinkled it with gasoline, threw a lighted match on it, and it soon ignited. The fire had to be coaxed to keep burning, but as he added small sticks and blew on the ignited wood, it was soon burning with gusto.

The roaring fire cheered him, and he began to feel more optimistic about his predicament. He had faith in the ability of the Coast Guard to find him, and there was little doubt in his mind that he would be rescued the next day. He even convinced himself that he might be found that night by some Mexican fisherman in the area who would see the glow on the beach.

When he returned to the plane to get his water bottle and some food, he decided to eat the last banana and several crackers for supper. He was so hungry that he could have easily eaten all that he had left, but he knew that it was necessary to be prudent.

The beach was now completely dark, and the flames leaping up from the fire were the only illumination to be seen anywhere. There were no lights from any boats offshore, nor were there any along the coast or inland. Steve felt as if he were isolated in a lonely world of his own.

He zipped up his jacket and settled down on the sand near the reserve wood. As he ate his meager ration he figured the number of hours that had passed since his last square meal. He had eaten breakfast in San Diego the morning before at 5

A.M. and nothing since except the food he had rationed himself from the plane. It had been thirty-eight hours, and it was no wonder that he was weak from hunger. He decided that he would try to catch some fish in the morning.

As the flames crackled and the night wore on Steve's thoughts again turned homeward. His parents did not yet know that Barbara's family were to announce the engagement in a few weeks. He had planned to telephone and surprise them with the news. They had not even met Barbara, but Steve intended taking her home with him when he spent Christmas in Chicago. He knew they would love her as he did.

He interrupted his thoughts to add more fuel to the fire. As he stood up he could see that the night tide was already lapping around the plane. His runway guides and signal letters had been obliterated long before, but he could renew them the next day at low tide.

To make himself more comfortable, he burrowed a place in the sand near the wood and prepared to keep a vigil as long as possible. In his weakened state he was finding it extremely hard to stay awake. The warmth of the fire was relaxing and soon his head was nodding. Shortly afterward his head fell forward on his chest, and he dropped off in a deep slumber.

The fire burned down slowly as he slept. At last it was merely a heap of glowing embers.

Sometime near midnight a moving form glided silently through the darkness toward the glow on the beach. Silently it crept nearer and nearer. Sudden sparks from the fire, as a dry twig caught, caused it to stop. Sensing no danger, it again moved closer and closer to the fire. Finally, sitting back on its haunches, it quietly observed the sleeping man, its sensitive nose and ears alert for any signs of danger. At a movement from the man, it poised for flight! But the man, still unconscious, had merely fallen over from a sitting position and now lay prone on the sand.

After an interval, the coyote resumed its cautious crawl toward the man. Its body tensed for any signs of danger, it crept nearer. As it circled the man its keen nose identified a familiar scent, a scent associated with food and kindness. It was not afraid now. This was not a danger scent. Satisfied, it moved away from the fire and sat down to watch the man.

Meanwhile the fire had nearly died. Only a few tiny embers still burned. The moon, which had risen earlier, now bathed the beach in its soft light.

Steve opened his eyes with a start. Although he was still exhausted, he knew that he should check on the fire. He sat up slowly and gazed with dismay at the feeble flames.

36   "I should get up immediately and try to get the fire going again," he told himself; but his inertia was too strong.

Instead he looked around at the unearthly beauty of the beach in the moonlight. Suddenly his heart took a jump! Sitting on the sand a few yards away was a big coyote. Its long tawny fur shone glossily in the moonlight, and its eyes sparkled like jewels as they reflected the light from the fire.

Steve's momentary fear left him as he and the animal stared at each other. He was aware that coyotes, aroused by curiosity or hunger, often came around camps at night. He imagined that the coyotes in Baja California were so unused to humans that they were less wary than those nearer civilization. Since this one seemed unafraid, he assumed that it was hungry, and he wished that he had some food to share. However, it looked well fed, so perhaps it was just curious. In the soft light from the moon it resembled a shepherd dog.

Turning his eyes back to the fire, Steve decided that he would have to get up and add some wood before it completely died out. He was not afraid that the coyote would attack him, for he had never heard of one attacking a man, but he hated to scare it away. As he got to his feet, the animal turned and loped away in the moonlight. Steve watched its graceful retreat over the dunes, its long bushy tail flying behind.

"Well, *adios*, Amigo," he called. Somehow he felt more lonely than ever as the coyote disappeared over the last visible dune.

He started the fire blazing again with more gasoline, and settling himself in the sand hollow, vowed to keep awake. As he sat immobile, watching the flickering flames, his thoughts returned to the coyote. The animal certainly was unlike any other coyotes he had seen while hunting in the California mountains. It was larger and healthier looking. Steve found himself wondering how it could find enough food and especially water on the dry and barren desert.

"It probably lives on rodents and shore birds," he decided. But he still could not figure out how it obtained drinking water.

Eventually he dozed as the long night wore on. His last thoughts before he finally fell into a deep slumber were that he would surely be in his own bed the following night.

Chapter 5

STEVE WAS AWAKE AS THE FIRST STREAKS OF DAWN appeared in the east. His bones and muscles ached, and he was shivering from his night on the sand. He was now so weak from hunger and thirst that he could hardly stagger to the plane for his ration of one orange. He was so dehydrated that he drank deeply from the water bottle.

His jacket and slacks were wet from the heavy dew that had fallen in the night, and he took them off and hung them on the plane wing to dry. As he did so, he noticed that the plane wing also was covered with dew. This gave him an idea.

"If I run out of water," he thought, "I can somehow collect the morning dew before it evaporates." But he quickly put the thought out of his mind. The possibility of remaining on the beach long enough to run out of water was too remote. He still had well over two quarts left.

Although he was hungry enough to attempt to catch a fish, he decided that it was more important to first replace the guiding marks of the runway and to gather more shells for the S O S letters. The

39

tide was going out, and the shells should be replaced as soon as possible to be ready for any passing plane.

As he gathered the shells and made the trip back and forth from the dry sand to the wet sand Steve thought over various ways in which he could capture a fish. He had a pocket knife, and he could sharpen the end of a stick and attempt to spear one. The main difficulty would be seeing one in the murky water and spearing it before it got away. He might as well try to grab one with his hands.

When he had finished filling in the letters again, he was so tired that he gave up all thoughts of fishing and sat down to rest. In his weakened condition it had taken him longer to do the job than it had the day before, and it was already the middle of the morning. The sky was as empty of aircraft as it had been on the preceding day.

Steve was forced to face the fact that if a rescue plane failed to appear that day, it would be best for him to leave the plane and scout around for help on his own. On the other hand, he knew that the country was so sparsely settled that he might have to walk across the desert for many miles before he found some remote ranch or tiny hamlet. He had no idea which direction he should take if he did attempt such a trip.

40   He got his air map from the Cessna. If he could only identify the beach he was on, he would know which way to start for one of the small habitations

marked on the map. However, there were scores of similar beaches along the coast, and he could only guess approximately where he might be.

Making the decision to stay by the plane was difficult. His tendency was to start walking and get someplace as fast as he could, but he knew this was foolhardy. He would have to have extra food and water to take along, or he might be worse off than he was already.

"At least I can walk back over the dunes a little way," he decided. It might be possible to get high enough to orient himself by some landmark, or he might even see some distant habitation. When he had landed during the storm, the clouds had obscured all but the beach.

Before starting off, he drank some water and scanned the sky thoroughly, but there was nothing but the usual flocks of gulls.

Walking up and down over the dunes was tiring, and Steve soon found that his depleted strength was ebbing. He was afraid to go too far for fear he would not be able to summon enough strength to make it back to the plane. Every step was becoming an effort, but the thought of seeing a column of smoke or some other sign of a ranch kept him going.

"I'll just drag myself up one more dune," he thought, "and if there is nothing to be seen I'll turn back."

His head was beginning to swim, and he felt

very faint as he crawled up the sliding sand. At the top he collapsed in a heap and had a momentary blackout. The sand he had dislodged at the top went on spilling down the other side.

After a few minutes, his head cleared enough so that he could look around. He was indeed on a higher dune, and he gazed unbelievingly at the scene that was spread out before him. Taking his sunglasses off, he rubbed his eyes and looked again.

Instead of the expanse of desert that he had thought was back of the dunes, he saw, not more than a mile distant, a great body of blue water. He could not estimate its size as the clouds covered the horizon.

"I'm so faint I must be seeing a mirage," he muttered to himself.

He closed his eyes to rest them, but when he opened them again, the water was still there. Between the dunes and the water, the land sloped down to a small beach with waves breaking on the shore. It was another pocket beach in the rocky coast similar to the one where the plane lay, but this one was much smaller. Turning in the direction he thought was north, Steve saw high brush-covered hills. He could not see what was beyond. When he turned south, it was the same. Turning back in the direction from which he had come, he saw the distant beach with the plane a mere speck on its long expanse.

"Where on earth am I?" he exclaimed aloud. "I've never seen this area on the map!"

As he looked carefully in all directions again he was more puzzled than ever. Even in his exhausted physical state, he knew that he was not having a hallucination. It was the real thing. He told himself that he must have missed something on the map that would identify the area.

Steve had never known a longer mile than he traveled getting back to his beach. He half crawled and half walked as he retraced his steps in the hot sun, but he knew he had to make it.

Over an hour later he crawled into the shadow of the plane wing and fell asleep from sheer exhaustion.

After a long interval, he came to and felt sufficiently revived to get up. He got his water bottle and the last orange. Rationing or no rationing, he knew that he was going to have to eat and drink to keep going. As he drank he noted that the bottle now contained less than two quarts. In the light of his puzzling discovery, this was alarming. The water might have to last him much longer than he had even dreamed.

Unfolding his air map, he sat down to scrutinize every inch as carefully as possible. He examined it meticulously, but he failed to find any area that conformed with the layout he had seen from the dune. There was nothing on the Pacific Coast to match it. Although Scammon's Lagoon was full of branching waterways and a small flat island, there was nothing on the map like the body of water he had seen.

He even examined the coast of the Gulf on the other side of the peninsula. He knew that it was most improbable that the plane could have blown the entire width of the peninsula, but he had to find some solution for what he had seen. There were large islands in the Gulf, but they were too far north or too far south.

The big island of Cedros, which was about thirty miles off the Pacific Coast, was near Guerrero Negro, and Steve knew that he could not be that far north or west. Besides, it had a good-size settlement, and he had seen no evidence of any people from the dune. And, too, it was mountainous and not as narrow in any place as the area between the two beaches.

As he discarded one place after another, Steve was more puzzled than ever. He tried recalling the scene from the dune in detail.

"Could it be possible that this is a small island off the Baja coast?" he asked himself. There were none, except Cedros, marked on his map, but he knew that there were several remote small ones that were never shown on air maps.

Steve pondered the startling possibility that he might be stranded on an island.

Chapter 6

||||||||||||||||||||||||||||||||||||||||||||||||||||||||||||||||||||||||||||||||||||||||

AS THE AFTERNOON PASSED STEVE'S MORALE SANK lower and lower. He could no longer hope for an early rescue. If he was stranded on an island, as he suspected, it could be weeks before he was discovered. He knew that the air search would be concentrated on and near the Baja coast, where his route was known. It would probably never occur to anyone that the storm could have blown him so far out to sea, or if it did, that he could possibly have landed on one of the small islands. If he was not found within a reasonable time, the assumption would be that he had perished in the ocean during the storm.

"I can't panic," he thought grimly. "I've got to survive somehow."

The situation seemed so hopeless that he was tempted to do nothing but wait for some fishermen to come near enough to the island to see the wrecked plane and investigate. At the moment, that seemed to be the only chance he had. However, he knew that this was a dangerous attitude. If he did not get busy and find food and water, he might not live long enough to be rescued.

Food was of prime importance. He still had water, but he had very little food left. A half-box of crackers and the two candy bars were all that remained. It was enough to keep him alive for quite a long time, but not enough to build up the strength he would need to explore the brush-covered hills he had seen from the dune. It was necessary to find out as soon as possible if he really had landed on an island. Until he knew, he had no way of calculating his chance of survival.

He began to think of ways to catch fish with what he had available. A sharpened stick was impractical. He could never get near enough to spear a fish with such a crude implement, and if he could, the point would probably break at the impact. If he only had some kind of hook and line, there were plenty of sand crabs available for bait. Perhaps the Cessna contained something with which he could fashion a line.

Suddenly he remembered that he had not looked in the plane's luggage compartment since the crash. He had forgotten what it contained besides a toolbox.

He ran quickly to the plane and pried open the compartment door. There was his toolbox and back of it was a coil of light nylon rope, a large spool of thin wire, and a gallon of oil for the engine. He pulled everything out and examined the compartment again. In a corner was his metal first-aid kit, which he kept for emergencies.

He opened it and investigated its contents. It contained packages of different-sized bandages, a roll of gauze, some adhesive tape, a roll of cotton, a bottle of disinfectant, a tin of aspirin, a tube of ointment, and a container of sulfa powder. But there was nothing that would be useful in catching fish.

He picked up the nylon rope and the spool of wire. He decided to use a length of the rope as a line and to fashion a hook from the wire. His tool-box contained a pair of pliers, as well as a screw-driver, a set of wrenches, and a small hammer. With the pliers he would be able to cut off a piece of the wire and bend it into a small hook.

Before making the fishline, he decided to bolster his flagging energy with one of the candy bars. Nothing had ever tasted so delicious. He was tempted to eat the other but controlled himself.

He opened his pocket knife and cut off a long piece of rope. Next he fashioned a makeshift hook and barb out of a piece of the wire. He knotted the rope securely through a loop in the upper part of the hook, and it was ready for the bait. To keep the hook from floating on the surface of the water, he wired a heavy piece of shell near the end of the line.

When he had finished, he dug up several of the

mole crabs that burrowed in the wet sand at the surf line. Their shells were soft, and they could easily be attached to the wire hook.

The small fish were again running shoreward, and this was a good indication that the larger fish in deeper water were hungry. A few of the sardines, in their frantic escape to keep from being eaten, had been carried to shore by the surf and were stranded when it retreated. If the soft sand crabs were not good bait, Steve decided he would try some of the sardines, either for bait or to eat.

Now he was ready to try his luck at catching a meal. He coiled the rope line in his hand and, stepping into the surf up to his knees, cast the line as far out as it would go. He had used about thirty feet of rope and it extended beyond the first breaker. When the crab-baited hook hit the water, it sank down out of sight, pulled by the weight of the shell.

As he waited patiently for a nibble Steve noted that time had passed quicker than he realized. The sun was setting, and he knew that he would have to catch a fish shortly or it would be dark before he got his fire going.

After fifteen minutes of fruitless waiting, he decided to change the bait. Perhaps a sardine would be better. After all, the fish were still chasing them inshore. If they were feeding on sardines, it would be better to use the same thing.

He pulled in his line and picked up one of the stranded sardines that appeared to still have some life. He attached it to the hook and cast the line out once again.

Before long he felt a nibble, then another. He was afraid to jerk the line for fear the wire barb was not sharp enough to catch hold.

Although his hand was shaking with excitement, he held the line steady and waited to see if the fish would take the bait again.

"It would be better if it swallowed the sardine," Steve cautioned himself. That way he could be sure it would not get away.

In a minute he felt another nibble; then came a strong jerk that almost pulled the rope from his grasp. As the fish took off with the hook and line Steve forced himself to keep from pulling it in immediately. He walked in and out of the water trying to tire the fish as he gently drew it closer. He had no idea what kind of creature was on the end of the line, but he prayed that it would remain secure.

For ten minutes he played the line cautiously back and forth, then it was suddenly still.

"It's gotten away," he thought desperately. He started to draw in the line, but as he did so, he felt a heavy object on the end.

"It's still there!" he yelled excitedly, as he very carefully pulled the line up through the surf

49

into the shallow water. Now he could see something white on the end. It was not struggling at the moment. He pulled it closer and closer. At last the fish emerged from the water onto the wet sand. When it felt the air, it began to lunge and try to head back into the surf.

"No, you don't," Steve yelled, and he threw down the rope and flung himself on the fish before it could detach itself from the hook.

Grasping the slippery creature with both hands, he held it up jubilantly. Luck was with him. It was a foot-and-a-half-long corbina, one of the best food fish to be found in shallow water.

Steve could hardly wait to get his fire started and cook the fish. He felt that he would even eat it raw if necessary.

Chapter 7

||||||||||||||||||||||||||||||||||||||||||||||||||||||||||||||||||||||||||||||||||||||

THE SUNSET GLOW WAS FADING AS STEVE GOT HIS matches and the shellful of gasoline from the plane. He started the fire as he had done the night before and was gratified to see the wood catch quickly after it had dried another day in the sun.

While cleaning the fish with his knife he thought of various ways to cook it. He had no pan in which to fry it, but he could make a grill of woven wire and suspend it above the coals. However, he was too hungry to take the time to make one. The quickest method was to impale the fish on the sharpened end of a stick and hold it near the coals.

When the fire had burned down sufficiently, he held the fish over the intense heat, turning it often to cook it evenly. It began to sizzle, and a wonderful smell filled the air.

He had been so engrossed in cooking and in anticipating the meal that he had been oblivious to anything else. As he turned the fish for the last time he became aware that he was being watched. He glanced around.

Behind him, not more than fifteen feet away, he saw the coyote that had visited him on previous nights. It was watching the fish and licking its chops.

Again Steve felt no fear. He could see that the animal was only interested in the fish and meant him no harm.

"I know how you feel, old boy," Steve said aloud, "but I've got to have it to keep alive."

At the sound of Steve's voice, the coyote moved away and took a post a little farther from the fire.

Finally the fish was done. Steve could hardly wait for it to cool before he started devouring the succulent flesh. He felt guilty, for as he stripped the meat from the bones with his fingers, the coyote sat watching him intently.

As soon as his empty stomach was filled, Steve sat back with a sigh of content. His stomach had shrunk considerably during his scanty diet of the last three days, and he could not eat as much of the meat as he thought. He knew that he would be sick if he ate any more that night.

Glancing toward the coyote, he made a quick decision. Why not share his meal? He knew that he should save the rest of the fish for the next day, but for some reason he felt a strange affection for the wild creature.

"Here, Amigo," he called softly, giving the animal the name which seemed to suit it best. He held up the remainder of the fish.

The coyote stood up, ears alert as Steve called, but it did not move.

"Come on, friend," Steve coaxed, but still the coyote kept its place.

Steve tossed the piece of fish toward the animal. It landed on some wood halfway between them. "It's yours, Amigo," Steve said quietly, "but you'll have to come and get it."

He could see that the coyote was eager for the food. It kept licking its chops, but it still seemed wary of coming closer to the man and the fire.

After an interval during which Steve sat quietly without moving, the coyote walked over to the fish and gulped it down. Then, without a backward glance, it trotted off in the dark.

The few seconds that the animal had remained in the light of the fire had enabled Steve to observe it closely. Around its neck he had seen the remnant of a crude handmade leather collar. He was greatly surprised to see this evidence of human contact on a wild animal. Steve began to wonder if it could be the pet of some Mexican fisherman. If so, there was probably a camp not far away.

On the other hand, he told himself, the animal might have been abandoned or perhaps it had escaped. It could have been taken from some litter as a small pup and raised as a pet. This would explain its bravado in approaching the fire.

"But," he asked himself, "if this is an island, how could it be here unless it was brought ashore in a boat?"

He resolved to get started as early in the morning as possible and explore some of the area that he had seen from the dune. He had to know if he was on an island and if there were any people in the vicinity. If he was on an island, it was necessary to know how far it was from the mainland. The closer it was to the coast, the better chance he would have of finding fishing boats or camps.

Tomorrow he would also search for water. His supply was becoming dangerously low, and he estimated that he had little more than a quart left. If he was unable to find a camp or a supply of water, he would have to try to collect the morning dew. He could mop it up with his tee shirt and wring the moisture into a shell, then pour the liquid into the bottle. It would be a long time before he had any large amount, but it would be better than nothing.

"Another thing that I will need," he reminded himself, "is food to take with me tomorrow." He chided himself for being so stupid as to give the rest of the fish away. The coyote, he knew, was perfectly able to find its own food. He did not regret his generous act, however, for the presence of the animal had given his morale a boost.

As he added more wood to the fire he decided

that it would be wise to try to catch another fish that night while the fire was still burning. He could cook it before he went to sleep, and it would be ready to take along in the morning.

The moon had not risen as yet, and it was pitch dark down at the water's edge. With a burning brand from the fire, Steve was able to see well enough to pick up another of the stranded sardines. He attached it to the hook and threw the line into the black waves. It was so dark that he could not tell where the line landed. He could only hope that something would bite.

The moon, rising late, found Steve still standing on the sand working his line in and out of the surf. Luck, however, was not with him this time. Either the fish were not biting, or the dead sardine was no lure.

Finally he gave up for the night. With a full stomach, he did not feel so desperate as he had earlier. He would try again in the morning.

Steve decided to sleep in the plane to avoid the dew. Before leaving the fire, he added a large supply of fuel to keep it burning as long as possible. He was worried about finding enough wood if he were to be on the beach for a long period, but that bridge could be crossed when he came to it.

He made himself as comfortable as possible in the cabin and began to think of home as he waited for sleep to come. He could easily imagine the newspaper items about his disappearance. "Coast Guard hunts lost flier in Baja. . . . When last seen, he was leaving La Paz on his way back to San Diego. . . . Presumed to be lost in the storm. . . ." Steve had read the same news about other pilots who had been forced down on the peninsula. They had always been found eventually, either dead or alive. He knew that the search for him would continue for a long period. Even pilots with private planes in the San Diego area would be called to join the Coast Guard in trying to locate him. The trouble was that it would never occur to any of them to look for him on an island, if, indeed, he was actually on one.

Although he hated to admit it to himself, he knew that if he was on an island any distance from the mainland, the rescue forces would have to give up in due time. It was only natural that they would assume that he had gone down in the sea. Such a freak accident as had happened to the Cessna could only occur once in a hundred years or never again.

Steve wished with all of his heart that he could spare Barbara and his parents the ordeal of not knowing his fate. It would help if they could only know that he was, at least, alive.

"Tomorrow I'm going to start hiking all over this area," he told himself with finality. "I've got to know where I am and what I'm up against."

Chapter 8

|||||||||||||||||||||||||||||||||||||||||||||||||||||||||||||||||||||||||||||||||

THE SARDINES WERE ACTIVE AGAIN EARLY NEXT morning when Steve threw his baited hook into the waves. This time he was lucky. He had an immediate strike, and he pulled in a fish which he assumed was a young halibut. It was good to eat, but he was hoping for another big corbina.

He walked in the surf to hip depth, carrying his line baited with another sardine. The water was quite clear, and he could see several large fish after the sardines. The incoming surf was surging against his body, but he managed to stand firm as he cast the line as close to the fish as possible. Soon he felt a mighty jerk on the line, but then it was slack again.

He was just about to pull in the line to see if the fish had taken the bait off the hook when he felt another tremendous jerk.

"Swallow the bait, swallow it," he prayed as he twisted the line around his wrist. He played the line back and forth carefully with both hands. His arms were becoming tired, but he did not dare give up, for the fish was still fighting to get away.

At last the fish was quiet, and Steve pulled it carefully toward shore as he backed out of the water. It was a much bigger corbina than he had caught the night before. As he drew it through the shallow water it began to fight again to get off the hook.

Steve threw down the line and ran into the water. He grabbed the fish, but it slipped from his grasp. Quickly opening his knife, he flung himself in the water and landed on top of the wriggling body just as it freed itself from the hook. He thrust his blade in as deep as it would go.

As he picked up the dying fish he guessed its size. It was two feet long and probably weighed nearly four pounds. It would furnish him food for several meals.

The sensible thing was to cook the two fish while they were still fresh, although it meant lighting the fire again and delaying his exploration of the area. But Steve knew that he ought not to start out without some food.

When the two fish were done, he ate a piece for breakfast and wrapped another piece in his handkerchief to take along. The rest he stored in his toolbox, which he closed tightly and buried in the wet sand near the plane. It was the only way he could think of to keep the fish from spoiling in the heat of the day.

To protect himself from further sunburn he put

on his tee shirt and rubbed his face and arms with some of the ointment in his first-aid kit. After a long satisfying drink from his water bottle, he was ready to leave the beach. The small amount left in the water bottle was alarming, but he was hoping to find a fisherman's camp or, failing that, some kind of spring back in the hills.

He had decided to explore the area north of the beach first. In his view from the dune these hills had looked higher than those to the south, and he figured they would give him a more extensive picture of the surrounding country.

Halfway down the beach, he turned back to look at the Cessna. He was not sure whether it was wise to leave the plane in the event that some pilot flew over the beach. However, he assured himself that the overturned plane would indicate that he was in the vicinity, either dead or alive. The S O S was still visible, and the remains of the fire were evidence that he had survived the crash.

At the end of the beach, the sand gave way to large rocks and low eroded cliffs. The tide was down, and Steve skirted tide pools left in the rock depressions by the receding water. Some of the pools were small; others were deep in the crevices between the rocks. He made a mental note to search the tide pools later for crabs and lobsters.

When he left the tide-pool area, he was forced

to climb upward as the coast became more rugged. As he climbed higher and higher he kept a look-out for ships at sea or planes overhead. Far down below him the waves dashed against the rocks and the weathered sandstone cliffs. Inland, the cliffs merged into brush-covered hills.

After he had covered about a mile and a half of the rough terrain, Steve's thirst began to bother him. He thought what a fool he had been not to bring his water bottle. The sun and the effort of climbing caused him to perspire, and he was losing precious body liquids at a fast rate. He soon realized that he would have to turn back or take a chance that he would find a spring. The fact that the hills were brush-covered made him optimistic about finding water. Vegetation required water to live.

He kept doggedly on, for he was determined to find out if he had landed on an island. A higher hill loomed in the distance inland, but after a while he realized that he probably could not make it that day. He was too weak from thirst.

He sat down on the top of the cliff to rest and to make up his mind whether he could continue or not. The breeze was blowing on top of the cliff, and he took off his shirt to cool his overheated body.

60   Suddenly his ears caught the sound of barking over the roar of the waves on the rocks below. It was a faint high-pitched barking and sounded like

a dog with a cornered rabbit.

Steve sprang to his feet. Could it be a dog? If so, it meant that the dog's owner was probably in the vicinity. He listened carefully to try to determine the direction from which the sound came. It seemed to be located about a quarter of a mile inland, back in the hills.

He forgot his thirst as he hastened toward the sound of the barking, which had continued at intervals since he had first heard it. The land sloped upward as he made his way inland, and the soil was dotted with cactus plants and low wind-blown bushes.

Steve could hardly contain his excitement as he puffed up the incline. If the dog was with someone, it meant that he was near some kind of human habitation.

Breathing hard as he reached the top of the low ridge, Steve looked down on the other side. Halfway down the slope he saw the animal. It was not a dog but his coyote friend. As Steve came over the ridge, the coyote stopped its barking but stayed where it was.

Steve's disappointment was bitter. He had convinced himself that help was around the corner, and he felt completely let down. He realized that he should have suspected that the barking came from a coyote. The idea of a dog was just wishful thinking.

He sat down to rest again and gather his resources together for the trip back to the beach. It was going to be a real test of his endurance to make it back without water.

As he rested he watched the coyote. It had completely ignored his presence and seemed to be concentrating on something among the rocks on the side of the hill.

"It probably is waiting to pounce on a cornered lizard or rabbit," Steve thought as he watched the animal.

Although he was exhausted, his curiosity got the better of him, and he approached closer to see what was attracting the coyote's attention. As he came near, the animal turned away and ran down the hill.

"If there's a rabbit in there maybe I can catch it myself," he thought as he knelt down and peered between the rocks.

There, protected by an overhang and deep within a fissure in the rock, was a pool of water!

Steve felt as if he had discovered a pot of gold. He leaned down and thrust his hands and arms in the cool clean water. He cupped his hands and drank and drank until he could hold no more. The water tasted like nectar in his parched mouth. He took off his shirt and soaking it with water sponged off his face and chest.

Now that he felt revived, he sat down beside the pool to eat the piece of fish he had brought. As he ate he wondered how the water happened to be in the cleft. It was not a spring, for there did not seem to be any source. He concluded that it must have drained down the slope the day of the storm and collected in the fissure. The overhanging rock had kept the sun from evaporating it.

Steve was very much refreshed after quenching his thirst and eating, but he decided that it was more important to get some of the water back to the beach than to tackle the climb up the hill in the distance. This seemed to be the highest point in the area, and it was from its summit that he hoped to be able to orient himself. But he would have to leave that job for the next day.

The problem of getting some of the water back to the beach faced him now. He mentally calculated the amount of water in the pool. He estimated that it must contain nearly seven or eight gallons. It was too bad to fill only his gallon bottle. What else could he use? All at once he remembered the old bottles in the debris on the beach. He would rinse some of them and carry more water back.

Before he started his return trip, he tied his white handkerchief on a bush to mark the site.

As he retraced his steps to the beach Steve realized what a debt of gratitude he owed his coyote friend. The animal had practically saved his life by attracting him to the pool.

Chapter 9

‖‖

IT WAS EARLY AFTERNOON WHEN STEVE RETURNED to the beach. He plunged into the ocean for a quick and refreshing dip, and then he started searching for bottles in which to store the water. There were several kinds scattered over the dry sand, and he chose an old gallon jug and four quart liquor bottles. These, when full of water, would be all he could manage to carry back.

The bottles were filled with sand and algae growth, and he had to rinse them several times in sea water to cleanse them thoroughly. Next he pulled off some cotton from the roll in his first-aid box. He planned to stopper the bottles with wads of cotton to keep them from spilling on the return trip. To facilitate carrying the bottles, he tied his jacket knapsack fashion on his back.

As he retraced his steps to the pool Steve hurried along at a fast pace. The afternoon was passing, and he was anxious to get the water back to 64 the beach before dark.

When he reached the hill and climbed to the top, he saw his handkerchief down the slope on the bush where he had tied it. The coyote was not at the pool nor were there any other animals visible, although Steve was certain that the pool must furnish water for a number of them.

When he had filled the jug and the bottles, he breathed a sigh of relief. He now had over two gallons of water, enough for several days, and there was plenty left in the pool for the animals.

On the way back to the beach, Steve paused to rest on the cliff. The bottles were heavy, and he shifted them to the ground and sat down on a rock. Shading his eyes from the afternoon sun, he scanned the ocean. Not far out he spotted a freighter, but it was too far away for him to attract its attention. It was comforting to see a sign of civilization, but he watched it with longing as it plowed its way across his line of vision.

"Why haven't I seen any planes or fishing boats?" Steve asked himself. He knew that there was no commercial passenger line serving the Pacific side of the Baja peninsula, but occasionally private planes flew over the vicinity of the coast. It was strange that he had not heard a single engine in the four days since the crash. This fact only increased his belief that he was stranded on an island. Tomorrow it was absolutely essential that he do some exploring.

When Steve arrived back at the beach, the sun was getting ready to set. He stored the water bottles in the plane and gathered a fresh supply of driftwood for his nightly fire. When he had finished, it was still warm enough for a final dip in the ocean.

As he entered the surf, pink from the glow of the setting sun, he was pleasantly surprised to see his coyote friend on the beach about a hundred yards away. It was standing in the water and seemed to be watching something in the surf.

His heart lifted at the sight of his friend. He was curious to see what the animal was doing, and he walked toward it. As he approached, the coyote gave him a look, then again turned its attention to whatever was in the water.

Steve was puzzled, and he stepped nearer to see what was so fascinating. All at once the coyote's paw flew out like lightning, and it slapped at something in the surf. In a second it had grabbed the thing in its jaws and was carrying it up on the sand. Steve followed at a safe distance. When it reached the sand, the coyote dropped its prey.

Now Steve could see a large crab that was still waving its menacing claws. With a low growl, the coyote pounced on the crab again. Avoiding the pincer claws, it shook it back and forth. Finally the crab's movements ceased, and it was dead.

Steve fully expected the coyote to tear the crab to pieces and devour the meat, but instead it walked up on the sand and sat down. The crab still lay on the wet sand.

Steve was surprised that the animal had not even carried it away. Its attitude seemed to imply that it had enjoyed catching the crab but that it was not hungry.

The crab meat would make a delicious supper, but Steve was afraid to pick it up, afraid that the coyote was playing a game and would pounce on him if he did.

He turned and walked back to the plane, leaving the crab where it lay. As he dressed he was sorry that he had not picked it up; however, since he was not sure of the coyote's intention, it was better not to chance an attack.

When he was dressed, he started his fire and settled down to eat a piece of the fish he had stored that morning. Night had fallen, and he was feeling desolate and lonely. He was thinking of Barbara and wishing that he was home when he heard a low whine nearby in the darkness.

He called softly, "Come here, Amigo." He was pleased that the animal had no fear of him.

At the sound of Steve's voice, the coyote emerged from the dark into the circle of light made by the fire. In its mouth was the dead crab. As Steve watched, it dropped the crab on the sand, then turned and was swallowed up in the darkness again.

Steve was puzzled. He kept himself from making any quick movement as he called to the coyote again. But, apparently, it had no intention of returning.

Steve pondered over the action of the animal in bringing the crab to the fire. He had fully expected it to settle down and eat the crab, but on the other hand the coyote could have been giving it to him as a gift. He laughed at himself for crediting an animal with generosity, but no other solution seemed plausible at the moment.

"Well, I'm not going to turn down a gift whether it was intentional or not," he decided. The crab meat would be a most welcome addition to his diet.

He stood up and stepped cautiously over to the crab. He was still not going to take any chances until he was sure that the coyote had abandoned it. Stooping over, he slowly picked it up and waited tensely to see if the coyote would return. When the animal failed to reappear, he was no longer afraid.

He examined the crab. It was a large rock crab and had probably come from one of the tide pools at the end of the beach. It was still fresh and would make a delicious meal if he could boil it in sea water and remove the shell. But he had no pot of any kind.

68 He thought over the things he had seen in the beach debris, but he could not recall seeing a vessel of any kind. Suddenly it occurred to him

that he could use the oilcan in the plane. First it would be necessary to empty the oil in beach bottles, and then he would cut off the top of the can with his knife and attach a wire handle.

He spent the rest of the evening making the pot. With the combination of his knife and the pliers and screwdriver from his toolbox, he was able to transform the oilcan into a pretty good kettle. Getting rid of the residue of oil was his biggest problem. After pouring the sticky liquid in beach bottles, he scrubbed the can with sand and washed it repeatedly with sea water. Finally, to remove the last traces of oil, he filled the can with more sea water and put it on the coals to boil.

As he waited for the water to boil he kept a watch for the coyote, but it did not return. Steve concluded that it must have gone back to its lair for the night. He fell to musing about the animal. Did it have a mate? He had not seen any other coyote, but there certainly must be others in the area.

When the oilcan was clean, Steve filled it once more with sea water and put the crab on to boil. By this time, he was quite weary. It had been a long day and he was sleepy, but he was eager to taste the crab meat. When it was cooked and he had stripped away the shell, he had the best meal he had eaten since he had crashed on the beach.

Chapter 10

THE NEXT MORNING STEVE AWOKE SOMETIME NEAR dawn. It was still dark, but a partial moon made a path of light on the ocean. He had stretched out near the fire the night before and fallen asleep. He was shivering, and he sat up to see if there were any live coals remaining.

As he became accustomed to the half-light, he saw a curled-up form a few yards away. There was no doubt what it was. It was Amigo. He had burrowed in the warm sand and was sound asleep.

Steve was touched. It was evident that the coyote trusted him, or it would never have relaxed to such an extent in his presence. He no longer felt so lonely as he looked at the sleeping animal. He wished that he could call it to him and fondle it as he would a dog, but he knew that it was best to let it make the first gesture of friendship. Its natural instincts would keep it at a distance until it felt sure of his intentions.

70 As he meditated on this odd new relationship Steve dropped off once again into a sound sleep.

He was awake as the first rays of the rising sun

warmed the beach. His limbs were cramped, and his clothes were again wet with dew. He looked for the coyote, but it had gone.

After drying his clothes and breakfasting on left-over fish, he was ready to follow his plan to climb the high hill beyond the pool. This time he carried a bottle of water as well as a portion of the crab meat from his late meal of the night before. He had no intention of suffering from thirst or hunger again.

By nine o'clock he had retraced his steps of the previous day as far as the turn-off to the water pool. Instead of turning inland, he continued along the top of the palisades, which became higher and more precipitous as he made his way toward the distant hill. Down below the cliff walls, the coast was rocky and inaccessible to anyone approaching from either land or sea. It was a long drop to the bottom of the cliffs, and Steve picked his way carefully. A fall could end disastrously.

Every few minutes he stopped to scan the sky and the ocean for planes or ships, but a distant column of smoke from a ship was all that he saw, and it was so far off that he could hardly see it.

After he had traveled for another hour, Steve suddenly had the feeling that he was being followed. Stopping short, he turned around and looked back. A few yards to the rear he saw the coyote.

"Hi, Amigo," he called. "I hope you don't mind if I explore your territory."

As Steve spoke the coyote sat back on its haunches. With its pointed ears alert and its slanting eyes watching the man, it seemed to be waiting for something.

"Now what do I do?" Steve thought. He wanted to walk over to the animal and pat its head, but he was afraid to hurry any familiarity. He also still had some reservations about the coyote's intentions toward him.

He quietly eased himself onto the ground and waited to see what would happen. It was up to Amigo now.

In a few minutes the coyote seemed to have made a decision, for it moved over to Steve and lay down beside him. Steve felt a thrill at this final gesture of trust from a wild animal. He no longer had any misgivings about the coyote's intention. He moved out his hand slowly and began to stroke the glossy fur gently. The coyote made no objection, and Steve continued. The expression of affection seemed to release some of Steve's pent-up emotions of the last few days, and he found himself feeling a great fondness for the animal. As if to seal the bond of mutual friendship, the coyote licked his hand, and its tail moved back and forth in pleasure.

"Now, it's time to get going," Steve said gently.

As he stood up he was not sure what the coyote

would do. Would it follow him, or would it go off on its own? But when he started off, there was no doubt. It followed as docilely as a dog.

Before long, Steve decided to turn inland. The hill that he planned to climb was not far away, and there were a series of ridges and small canyons to cross before he started the actual ascent to the top. The hill appeared much higher than when he had seen it in the distance from the dune.

By noon, he was hungry. He was near the steep slope of the hill, but he decided to rest before continuing on. He sat down beside a low bush and unwrapping the crab meat from his handkerchief began to eat. The coyote had lain down nearby, and he decided on impulse to share the food.

"I guess we're in on everything together from now on, fellow," he said to the animal as he laid part of the crab meat on the ground.

The coyote pricked up its ears as he spoke but was in no hurry to take the food.

"It's for you, Amigo," Steve coaxed. "Come on and get it."

Finally the animal walked with dignity to the food, swallowed it one gulp, and returned to its resting place.

Steve was sorry not to share his water, but he had no receptacle in which to pour it. He knew that the coyote could obtain water at the pool if it was thirsty.

His energy restored by the food and water,

73

Steve continued on. Now he began to see clumps of various cactus plants as well as a variety of small shrubs which became thicker and thicker the farther inland he went. Soon he noticed that some of the large cactus plants had fruitlike protuberances growing on the end of the pear-shaped lobes. All at once he realized that this must be prickly pear. He had heard that the fruit was edible. If so, he had made a discovery of value, a welcome addition to his diet of fish.

He was anxious to taste one of the fruits, but he saw that the plants, which grew in great clumps, were covered with sharp spines. The fruit itself was covered with tiny needlelike hairs, which could be very annoying if they came in contact with the skin.

Steve approached one of the bushes cautiously. He had no wish to come in contact with the sharp spines, but he was eager to get some of the fruit. Using his water bottle, he knocked several of the pale green podlike fruits to the ground. The soil was packed hard, and he rolled them over and over with the bottle to rub off the almost microscopic hairs. Finally, he picked one up gingerly. He peeled back the rind with his knife and tasted the fruit. It was full of seeds and juice. Although he had to spit out the seeds, the fruit tasted quite good and was thirst-quenching. He ate several, then wrapped his handkerchief around a few others before storing them in his pocket. He had not been able to avoid getting some of the tiny needles in his skin, but although they were irritating, they were not big enough to do any damage.

Half an hour later Steve began the gradual climb up the hill. He hurried along, as the afternoon was passing and he did not want to spend the night away from the beach or to pick his way back along the cliffs in the dark. Halfway up he noticed that the coyote had not followed. He assumed that it had gone back to drink at the pool.

Before he reached the top of the hill, he was quite weary. However, the urge to see what lay beyond hastened his steps. Breathing hard from exertion, he stood at last on the summit and gazed around. Since the hill rose nearly one thousand feet above the rest of the land, he could see for miles.

Now Steve knew for certain that he was on an island! He saw that he was on the highest point of a long and narrow piece of land completely surrounded by water. The great open expanse of the Pacific Ocean lay to the west, and to the east, where he surmised the Baja peninsula lay, clouds were hovering. They were moving slowly, and as he looked they scattered enough for him to get a view of a long mass of land. Without a doubt it was the mainland, and it appeared to be at least forty miles away.

As he saw how far the island was off the coast,

Steve's mouth fell open in amazement. It was incredible that it could be so far away. How could the storm have driven him to the one island in the vicinity? And still more incredible, how could he have had the good luck to land on the island instead of in the sea?

As he marveled at the freakishness of the storm he looked over the layout of the island. It appeared to be about six miles in length and varied in width from about three miles at its widest part to about two miles at its narrow portion. In contrast to the narrow part, which was low and dune-covered, the rest of the interior of the island was high and covered with vegetation. The whole coast, with the exception of the two indented beaches on either side of the dunes, was rugged and inaccessible.

To the south, beyond the two beaches, Steve could see another smaller hill and still farther the rocky coast of the island's rounded tip. The north end of the island was the same except that the tip ended in a headland and a number of detached high rocks.

Once again Steve marveled at the capriciousness of the hurricane. There were no other islands nearby and at the moment not even a ship was visible in the distance. It was an isolated spot, but he had one thing to be thankful for. He was lucky that the storm had blown him to the larger beach

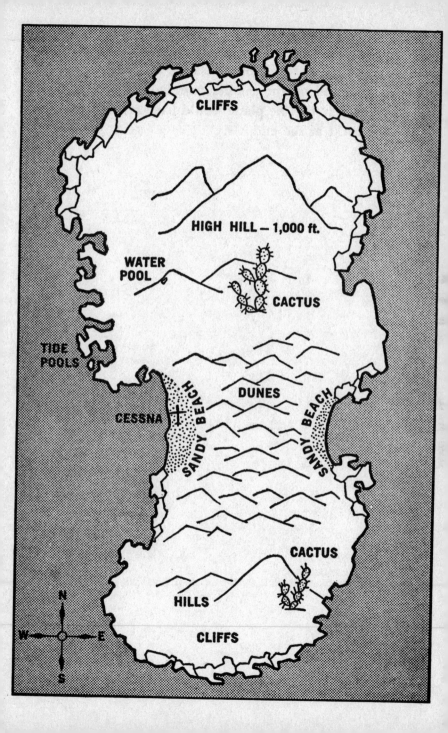

on the west side of the island. Had he been forced to land on the smaller one, he could never have survived. The plane would have crashed into the rocks at the end.

Chapter 11

||||||||||||||||||||||||||||||||||||||||||||||||||||||||||||||||||||||||||||||||||||||||||||||||||||||||||||

STEVE'S AMAZEMENT AT FINDING HIMSELF SO FAR
from civilization soon gave way to despondency.
He had little hope of being rescued by a plane.
He could hardly expect the searchers to look for
him on a remote island. His best chance was to
be picked up by some Mexican fishing boat. He
had not seen any so far, but it seemed impossible
that the island had never been used as a base for
fishing unless the fish in the vicinity were scarce.

He sat down on the hilltop to consider the
seriousness of his predicament. This was his fifth
day on the island, and there was the possibility
that he would have to stay a long time before anyone came ashore or a boat approached near enough
to signal. In the meantime there was the matter of
survival. That would have to be planned carefully.
For the present he had a source of food and water,
but what would he do when the water ran out?

"Well," he resolved, "I won't think that far
ahead."

As he reexamined the island from his vantage
point, he concluded that he must explore it

thoroughly to determine if fishermen had ever camped along the shore. If he found evidence that they had, then he would know that there was a chance that they might return.

Finally he decided that he would cross over the dunes the next day and look over the smaller beach for signs of a former camp. The two beaches were the only accesses to the island. The rest of the coast was too rugged for a safe landing in a boat.

While studying the island and concentrating on his plans Steve had been oblivious to the passage of time. With a start he suddenly realized that he had dallied on the hill too long and might not get back to the plane before dark.

He glanced at his watch. It was nearly 5:30. He was disgusted with himself for ignoring the time; he was aware that it would be dangerous to make his way along the cliffs after dark. It was not desirable to spend the night away from the beach for he had no food other than the cactus fruit. Also, he had not brought his jacket or even one match.

As he hurried down the steep hillside he tried as carefully as he could to avoid the spiny cactus plants. However, in his haste he tripped over a plant with particularly sharp needles, and some of them penetrated his shoe leather and pierced the flesh of his foot.

Begrudging the loss of time, he sat down on the ground and removed his shoe. The spines had lodged in his foot and were causing him considerable pain. As he removed the spines he noted with alarm that the sun had already dropped below the horizon. There was not time enough to get back to the beach before night. He would have to pick his way over the last part of the cliffs in the dark.

He put his shoe back on and got to his feet. When he started forward, he found that his foot was so sore that it would slow him up considerably.

Limping along as best he could, at last he came to the cliffs and turned south toward the beach. The twilight was already waning, and he estimated that only half an hour of daylight remained.

"Perhaps I should just sit out the night and wait until it's light enough to see my way," he told himself. "It will be cold and damp but better than risking my neck in a fall to the rocks down below."

While it was still light enough to see, Steve picked as sheltered a place as he could find. A small gully traversing the cliff top offered the best protection from exposure to the night breezes. As he settled himself in the shallow depression he was already shivering, but he consoled himself that it was better to catch cold than to risk a fall from the cliff. He could hear the waves thundering as they crashed on the rocks below, and as he visualized himself hurtling down the sheer wall of the cliff, he was glad that he had decided to wait until the next day to continue.

Soon it was pitch dark, and Steve sat huddled in the gully with his arms wrapped tightly around his chest to keep warm, thinking what a fool he had been not to bring his jacket. It was wind-proof and would have given him some protection from the cold wind blowing off the sea.

In an hour his teeth were chattering, and he was forced to stand and stomp up and down to keep warm. The thought of the hours ahead before daylight was almost more than he could bear. He was tempted to continue along the cliff in the dark, risk or no risk.

As he pondered whether it was wiser to stay in the gully or continue back to the beach he heard a barking in the darkness. He listened carefully.

"It must be Amigo," he thought happily. "He's found me again."

"Amigo," he called. "Here, boy."

In a few minutes he heard a rustling nearby, and his outstretched hand found the body of the coyote. He stroked its fur and tried to coax it down beside him, but he could sense that the animal was alert and tense. It had found him but seemed to have no intention of staying. It darted away and began barking again.

"What's the matter, fellow?" Steve called. When he spoke, the coyote returned to his side, but again it refused to relax.

Steve decided that the animal, for some reason, did not want to stay in the gully. Perhaps there was some peril which was invisible in the dark. "If there is," Steve thought, "I'd better get out too."

He was still loath to attempt the cliffs in the dark, but because of the intense cold and the possibility of some unseen danger, he decided to risk it. He would follow the coyote. It was sure-footed and was familiar with the area. Even on such a cloud-covered moonless night it could see in the dark.

As he stood up he had an idea. "Why not let Amigo lead me? I can take off my belt and loop it through his collar."

He called to the animal. It showed no objection when Steve felt for its collar and attached his belt. Steve reasoned that at sometime it must have been restrained by a rope or leash, for it still made no objection when he grasped the belt and followed it through the dark.

Since he had made up his mind to trust the coyote's instinct for danger, Steve groped his way along after it as carefully as he could, hoping that he would not make a misstep. As time went by his eyes became more accustomed to the dark, and he could walk without stumbling.

Although he was not positive where the coyote was leading him, he knew that he was on the cliffs, for he could still hear the waves pounding below. His wounded foot bothered him and he walked with a limp, but fortunately the coyote made no attempt to dash ahead.

He figured that an hour or more must have gone

by when he began to go downhill. Soon he was forced to climb over and around rocks, but he kept his hand on the belt and followed the coyote with confidence.

"This must be the rocky area between the cliffs and the beach," he thought with relief. If so, he was nearing the plane.

At last Steve breathed a sigh of relief as he saw and felt the sand underfoot. He could hear the surf rolling in and out, and he knew that the coyote had led him safely back to his beach. In a few minutes the plane loomed up in the darkness. It was a most welcome sight.

Steve released the coyote and patted it with affection. "Good boy," he said. When a warm tongue licked his hand, he knew that the animal returned his affection.

The tide had risen, and the plane was surrounded by water, but Steve waded in and groped in the cabin for his jacket and matches. He got his first-aid kit and a shell full of gas and taking them up on the dry sand found the pile of wood he had collected the night before. Soon he had a roaring fire going, and as he warmed himself, he looked around for the coyote.

"Amigo," he called. "Where are you?" But the animal had disappeared again. Steve was disappointed. He wanted to share some of his leftover fish as a reward for his safe conduct to the beach.

He supposed that, since the coyote hunted mainly at night, it had gone off to find its own food.

When his chilled body was warm again, he treated his injured foot with the antiseptic from his first-aid kit. The cactus wounds were not serious, and he thought that they would probably heal within a day.

As he sat by the fire and munched his piece of fish Steve felt the deepest loneliness he had known since he had landed on the island. He now had little hope for an air rescue, and the chance that a boat would approach the island within the next few days was slim. He felt an overpowering fear when he thought of trying to keep himself alive until help appeared. He was sure that he could get enough food, but what would he do for enough water? It might rain, but he could not count on it, for this was the dry season. There was the dew, and there was probably still some water in Amigo's pool. These were his only sources when the present supply ran out.

As he thought over the means for survival at his disposal Steve was deeply thankful for the Cessna. It would provide him with several things which he might need, such as more wire. It had many feet of control wire, and too, the metal in the wings and fuselage might be useful for something if he were forced to remain on the island any length of time. For clothing he had only what he was wearing: his warm nylon jacket, his tee shirt, cotton slacks, his undershorts, his shoes, socks, and belt. His small possessions were a wallet, knife, key ring, and a pen and pencil. The wallet contained nothing of value for survival, merely some bills, credit cards, and a driver's license.

He took out his box of matches and counted them. It was a small box and he had used some already. There were only twenty left, but he remembered seeing a cardboard folder of matches in the plane.

He waded through the surf to the plane and, searching the interior, found the folder, as well as two magazines and a newspaper that had been left behind by his passengers. He counted the matches in the folder. It was almost full; there were nineteen left. This was a stroke of luck, for he had to have matches for the fire. He had an ample supply of gas in the plane's two tanks, and with gas he could start fires easily as long as the matches held out.

Steve was so fatigued from the day's adventure that he settled down in the plane and drifted off to sleep immediately. It was just as well, for brooding over his plight could only make him feel more desolate and unhappy.

Chapter 12

IIIIIIIIIIIIIIIIIIIIIIIIIIIIIIIIIIIIIIIIIIIIIIIIIIIIIIIIIIIIIIIIIIIIIIIIIIIIIIII

IT WAS LONG AFTER SUNRISE WHEN STEVE OPENED his eyes the next morning. He had been dreaming that an airplane was flying down to the beach to rescue him, and he was reluctant to return to reality. When he finally roused from his torpor, he sat up with a start. Perhaps he really had heard a plane!

He was out of the Cessna in a flash and dashing up on the nearest dune. He scanned the sky, but the morning overcast was still thick, and nothing was visible. He listened intently, but there was no welcome sound of an engine.

Finally he was forced to admit to himself that his dream had been too vivid. In his depleted physical state it was natural to have hallucinations and to confuse them with the real thing. As a competent flier himself, he knew very well that no good pilot would venture this far from the mainland unless he had an amphibian plane and a reason for doing so.

Although he was aware that he had been fooled by his dream, Steve nevertheless was disappointed, and his spirits were very low as he walked back to the Cessna. It was only with a tremendous effort that he was able to prod himself into getting the fishline and into making a halfhearted attempt to catch his breakfast. There were no stranded sardines, so he baited his hook with a small piece of the leftover fish. He tossed it out into the surf, where it bobbed about for awhile. After fifteen minutes had passed and he still had no nibble, he decided to give up and try the tide pools. The tide was extremely low and it was the best possible time to investigate the area exposed by the receding water.

After fetching his oilcan pot he headed toward the rocks at the north end of the beach. When he reached them, he was gratified to see that he could easily walk over the area that was usually under water.

The best place to look for lobsters, abalones, and even small octopi was where the outgoing surf had been caught in deep crevices. He stopped at a deep pool. Seaweed grew around its sides, and the rocks were covered with attached sea anemones and crustaceans of various kinds. The anemones, small round flowerlike creatures, squirted water and closed up immediately when he stepped on them. Here and there a starfish was attached to the rocks, and tiny little crabs ran for cover as he approached.

The pool itself seemed empty of life except for small fish, which darted under rocks to hide. Steve was aware, however, that larger creatures lurked under the rocks too. He had brought a piece of the cooked fish, and he tossed it into the pool and sat down to see what would happen. He hoped that it would lure a wary octopus or a lobster from its hiding place. He sat motionless for a long time before his patience was rewarded. Finally he saw the antennae of two of the clawless Pacific spiny lobsters emerge slowly from under the rock. The creatures crawled along the bottom of the pool toward the piece of fish.

Letting himself down quietly, Steve thrust his hand into the pool. As he disturbed the water, the lobsters made for the protection of the rocks. He managed to grab one with his hands, and he lifted it out of the pool into the pot. He felt under the rock for the other, but it kept slipping from his grasp. At last, he had it too.

When the two lobsters were safely in the pot, he covered it with his jacket so they could not escape. He was elated over his success and could hardly wait to get back to the beach to cook them. It was best, however, to hunt for more while the tide was so low.

Moving on to another pool, he captured a tiny live crab, which he threw into the water. As it scurried away toward a rock, a small octopus darted out to seize it with its beaklike jaw. Steve thrust his hand in the pool to grab the octopus, but it was too quick for him and propelled itself backward under a rock where it discharged a cover screen of inky black fluid. Steve leaned over the pool and felt under the rock for the octopus. His hand came in contact with its tentacles, but it had fastened itself so securely to the rock with the powerful suckers on the under side of the tentacles that he was unable to detach it. Finally he gave up. He was not particularly eager to eat an octopus in any event. He had only heard that the Japanese considered the flesh of the tentacles a delicacy, and he had seen them catching small octopi in the tide pools near San Diego.

He decided to try one more pool before returning to the beach. This time he was lucky. He captured two more lobsters and added them to the pot. Now he had enough food for several meals.

When he arrived back at the beach, Steve rekindled the fire and let it burn to a hot bed of coals. He filled the pot with sea water and boiled the lobsters two at a time. When they had cooled, he stripped out the white tail meat and sat down to enjoy a portion of it as his first meal of the day.

By the time he had finished it was early afternoon, and he had yet to cross the dunes and explore the other beach. It was important to look it over before another day went by. There might be signs of recent occupation by fishermen or something else that might aid plans for getting away from the island.

The best thing, he decided, was to spend the night on the other beach. This would give him time to explore it thoroughly and to avoid the return trip across the dunes in the dark.

He gathered several things together to take with him. In the oilcan pot he put the rest of the lobster meat and the cactus fruit that he had picked the day before. In his jacket, which he again tied knapsack fashion on his back, he placed a bottle of water and a bottle of gasoline well-stoppered with wads of cotton and newspaper. He carried his shovel and his first-aid kit, and in his pants pockets he had the box of matches and his knife.

Again he found it difficult walking up and down in the deep sand of the dunes, but this time he had considerably more strength and a definite purpose.

The day had turned out to be very clear, and from the time he topped the highest dune he could make out the distant high mountains of the Baja peninsula. They looked tantalizingly near, but the distance was deceiving. He verified his earlier estimates that the peninsula was at least forty miles away, and more likely fifty.

It was mid-afternoon when Steve crossed the last low dune and approached the small pocket beach. He saw that it was similar to the beach on the other side but was only half as long and much more indented. At each end, rocky headlands extended from the eroded façade of a long line of cliffs.

He chose a place for a fire on the dry sand well above the high-tide mark. The beach was well supplied with driftwood, but there were no bottles, crates, or other debris from ships, as he had found on the other beach. This indicated that large ships seldom passed between the mainland and the island. Their regular course was farther out to sea.

As he gathered wood for the fire Steve kept his eyes open for any signs of a former camp. Near one end of the beach, in a sheltered spot, he found what he was looking for. Small pieces of charcoal, some rusty cans, and three empty turtle shells, blackened by fire, were evidence that turtle fishermen had come ashore sometime in the past. The fire remains were of long standing, and the cans had lost their labels, but they were undeniable proof that the beach had been occupied.

As he examined the remains of the camp Steve felt more hopeful for a rescue than he had since he discovered that he was on an island. He reasoned that if fishermen had camped there once, it was possible that they might return at any time.

The turtle shells were most interesting. Apparently the man or men had dined on turtle meat that had been cooked right in the shell. Marine turtles were fairly abundant in the waters off Baja California, and some of the Mexican fishermen made their living by catching them and sending them to the markets at Ensenada. Steve recalled seeing them bring the turtles ashore one morning in La Paz. The Mexicans told him that they made the catch from a small boat, which approached the creatures as they floated on the surface of the water. Special harpoons were used to capture them alive. Once the turtles were in the boat they were turned over on their backs, and in this position they were helpless.

Steve had never tasted a turtle steak, but he wished that he had one at that moment. However, he had no way of catching a sea turtle. As far as he knew, they only came ashore on rare occasions to lay their eggs.

He continued his search for more evidence of camps, but as closely as he combed the area, he found no further refuse. This was disappointing.

While he had been searching the beach for clues Steve came to the conclusion that he would be better off making his headquarters on this side of the island. It was nearer to the mainland, and there was more of a chance of his nightly fire being seen by a fisherman. The island was far too distant for the smoke to be seen from the Baja coast, but the glow from the fire might be seen from a passing fishing boat. If no one saw his fire and investigated the island, then Steve concluded that he would have to try to make a raft.

Constructing a seaworthy raft would be a tremendous project, but he had seen stacks of driftwood at the end of the other beach, and many of the pieces were heavy enough to lash together into a floatable platform. He had wire, and he had rope, and it might be possible to build a raft if he planned it carefully.

Daylight began to fade as Steve finished gathering driftwood for a fire. He dug one depression in the sand in which he stacked some of the wood and another depression for himself. He lighted the fire with a match and the gasoline that he had brought, and then he settled himself to keep a long vigil.

He missed Amigo. It was even more lonely on the strange beach, and the companionship of the coyote would be comforting. He wondered if it was back on the other beach.

When he had finished his meal of lobster and cactus fruit, he burrowed into the sand and made himself as comfortable as he could under the circumstances. It was cold, but with his jacket and the warmth from the fire he was not too badly off. It was still the end of summer, and the nights were not yet as cold as they would be later on. If he was forced to remain on the island for many nights longer, he thought, it would be necessary to build some kind of shelter. The Cessna provided shelter on the other beach, but here he would have to build something to protect himself from the wind and the dampness.

As the night wore on Steve began to dwell on thoughts of home. He wondered if he had been given up for dead by this time, as no trace of his plane had been found by the searchers. He had kept track of the days in his mind, and since this was the end of the sixth day, he figured it was already the second of September. He could hardly bear to think of the anxiety his parents and Barbara must be experiencing. He hoped that they still had faith that he would be found alive.

Finally he made a decision. If he managed to keep healthy and was able to find enough food and water, he would stick it out on the island for another week, hoping to be picked up by a fishing boat. If by the end of a week he had not been rescued, he would attempt to build a raft and get to the peninsula on his own. In the meantime he would move his things to this beach and construct some kind of a shelter. The rest of the time he would spend exploring the island.

Steve felt better when he had made these decisions. Soon he was drowsy, and it was effort to get up and replenish the fire. Before he was aware of it, his eyes had closed, and he was sound asleep in his sand burrow.

Chapter 13

||||||||||||||||||||||||||||||||||||||||||||||||||||||||||||||||||||||||||||||||||||||

A SERIES OF LOUD, HOARSE BARKS, PUNCTUATED BY the frantic yapping of a coyote, waked Steve the next morning. He sat up and listened to the noise, which seemed to come from the rocky point at one end of the beach. It sounded as if it might be a coyote fight, but he could not be sure. He decided to get up and investigate. One of the coyotes could be Amigo, and he might be getting the worst of the fight.

It was just light enough for Steve to pick his way to the top of the rocky promontory that jutted out into the water. Down on the other side he saw a series of cavelike openings at the base of the cliff. The holes had been made by heavy wave action over many years. The tide was very low, and a narrow sandy beach was exposed in front of the caves.

The noise of the fracas was coming from one of the larger caves. As it continued Steve climbed down to the sandy strip and ran to the cave mouth. He was a little apprehensive, for he was afraid to get involved in a coyote fight. On the other hand, he felt obliged to help Amigo if he could.

As Steve peered into the cave he saw that it was indeed Amigo who was growling and yapping at something cornered in the cave recess. At first Steve could not determine whether it was another coyote or some other kind of wild animal, but as the light penetrated farther into the cave, he was able to see clearly.

Back in the corner of the shallow recess were two sea lions. One was much larger than the other; they appeared to be a female and her pup. Both of the seals were emitting peculiar barking noises, and the larger animal was lunging at the coyote.

Steve hesitated to interfere in Amigo's affair, but he could see that both the larger seal and the coyote already had wounds and that blood was streaming down their bodies. It was evident that the seal had teeth as efficient as those of the coyote.

Steve was not sure of Amigo's motive in cornering the seals. Did he intend to try to kill one for food? Or had he first been attacked by the female who sensed danger to her pup? Or had a fight started over a fish which one was trying to get from the other? Steve had no way of knowing, but he made up his mind to try to coax the coyote away before the fight became too serious.

Standing directly in front of the cave opening, he called loudly, "Come, Amigo. Come boy." He had some of the lobster meat with him, and he held it up as he kept calling, "Come on, boy, come on."

The coyote apparently heard him, for its frantic barking ceased and it backed out of the cave growling. Its hackles were up, and its lips were drawn back exposing the long, pointed fangs.

Steve was frightened, but he held his ground and kept proffering the food. After all, the coyote was a wild animal, and in spite of past friendly overtures it might turn on him for interfering. However, it was soon clear that the animal meant him no harm, for as it discovered Steve its hackles subsided and it ceased growling.

Steve was relieved. He backed away from the cave still holding the lobster meat aloft. The coyote followed him. When Steve was well away from the cave, he placed the meat on a rock and called to the animal. Without any hesitation, it walked to the rock and ate the food.

As it walked it limped, and Steve could see that a huge gash on the shoulder was responsible. The cut was bleeding but appeared to be the only serious wound that the seal had inflicted.

"You're going to need some first-aid treatment, Amigo, old boy," Steve said aloud. "Come on with me and we'll see about it."

He started back over the rocky point hoping that the coyote would follow. At first it hesitated and glanced back at the cave. The seals were still inside, but the man's coaxing voice kept calling. Finally, the animal seemed to give up, and it turned and followed Steve.

From the top of the rocky point Steve saw the two seals emerge from the cave and make for the water as fast as their awkward flippers would take them. They soon disappeared in the waves. The coyote also saw them, but it made no move to cut off their retreat.

"Now I wonder why Amigo is no longer interested," Steve observed. "It can't be for love of me, so it must be that he's tired of the whole business."

The coyote followed Steve back to the campfire site. As he picked up his first-aid kit, Steve wondered if the animal would permit him to treat the wound on its shoulder. He decided to try anyway, as the coyote settled down on the sand and began licking its fur.

Taking the water bottle and his kit, Steve moved over to the coyote and sat beside it. First he patted its head and talked in a soothing voice. Then, as his fingers gently probed the wound, he kept alert for the slightest signs of antagonism. Although the animal winced, it made no move to harm Steve. It seemed to sense that he was trying to help.

Steve wished that he could spare enough water to wash the wound, but instead he soaked a piece of cotton with water and sponged off the blood and dirt. The gash was quite deep and long.

After he had cleaned the wound, Steve applied sulfa powder to the raw flesh. "There now, fellow," he said. "You leave it alone and you'll soon be as good as new." Fortunately, the cut was in a difficult place for the animal to lick.

Next Steve poured some water from the bottle into the oilcan and put it in front of the coyote. It seemed thirsty and drank a considerable amount. Steve watched the water diminish with mixed feelings. Water was precious, but he could not let his friend down when he could help.

The sun was now warming the beach, and Steve left Amigo and walked to the surf's edge. He gazed longingly across the intervening water at the mainland, which was just barely discernible.

"If I had a raft I would leave here this minute," he said with emotion. But he knew that his decision to await rescue for another few days was wise.

As he stood on the wet sand that the receding surf had exposed he noticed that thousands of tiny beanlike shells covered the beach. Picking some up, he examined them carefully. They were bivalves, and each was no bigger than the end of his thumb. He pried the two valves of one open with the tip of his knife. When he tasted the meat he found that it was quite good, something like a miniature clam.

"These must be donax," he said to himself as he examined them more carefully. He had seen people picking them up in quantities on certain beaches near San Diego, and he had been told that they made a good soup. If so, he had made a discovery.

He ran to get his oilcan and filled it with as many of the little shell-covered animals as it would hold. Then he added some sea water to keep them fresh. He was already anticipating the soup he would have when he returned to the other beach. Also, he was elated when he realized that the donax would be a steady source of food when he moved camp.

Steve spent the rest of the morning sitting on the highest point on the rocky headland at the end of the beach. He hardly took his eyes from the ocean, but no boat of any kind came into view. The mainland had gradually acquired a covering of clouds, and finally he could no longer see it. He was discouraged, but he still figured that being on the side of the island nearest the peninsula was his best bet. Also, if he did make a raft, it would be much better to launch it from the closest place to his destination.

It was time to start back to the plane. He had many things to move over the dunes when he changed his location, and he told himself that he had better get them ready, as well as get in a supply of food.

When Steve went to pick up the potful of tiny clams and his other belongings, he found that the coyote was no longer on the beach. He hoped that the animal would not injure itself further, for he knew that the cut was probably causing it difficulty in walking.

As he started to leave the beach it occurred to him that he should leave some kind of message to indicate his presence on the island. If any fisherman should come to the island while he was on the other side, it would be tragic if they left without even knowing of his plight.

He hunted around for two flat pieces of driftwood. He needed a short wide piece for a sign and a long narrow one for the post. When he found what he wanted, he made a crude sign with charcoal. He tried to recall some Spanish words, but his knowledge of the language was limited to what he required at the Baja airports and in the towns.

Finally he printed "ACCIDENTE AEROPLANO EN OTRA PLAYA." He did not know if he had used the right words, but he meant it to read, "Airplane accident on the other beach." Underneath he wrote in English, "HELP! MAN STRANDED ON BEACH ACROSS DUNES."

With the wire handle from the oilcan he attached the sign crosswise to the longer piece of wood. Then he dug a deep hole in the sand with his shovel and stood the sign securely upright. Then he tied his handkerchief to it to attract attention.

"That ought to be easily seen by anyone near shore or landing on the beach," he thought with satisfaction.

As he retraced his steps back to the plane Steve

planned his tasks for the following day. He had the small clams, but when he had consumed the soup, he would be out of food again. He would have to get in a supply of some kind the next day, either fish or something from the tide pools. Also, he must invent some device for catching dew. His present supply of water could not last too much longer. The bottle he had taken to the new beach was almost empty, but he still did not regret giving the coyote part of it.

As the coyote came to mind Steve began wondering where it was. The wound should be doctored again, and he hoped that the animal would appear by nightfall. As he recalled the sea lion episode he was not sure that he had been right in stopping the fight. He might be sorry, if food was scarce, that he had not captured and killed one of the seals for himself. But he knew that as long as he could catch fish and find lobsters or other food in the tide pools, he had no heart to kill any creature as appealing as a seal. Even if Amigo had intended killing a seal for food, Steve knew that there were plenty of other sources for the animal. It was expert at catching shore birds, and there were lizards and mice and probably rabbits on the island.

Steve continued thinking about the coyote as he trudged from dune to dune. He thought it was strange that he had not seen any others on the island, but then he had not explored it as yet. If there were others, how could they have gotten here from the mainland? Was it possible that Amigo was the only one? If so, he must have been brought in a boat by a Mexican fisherman. This seemed the only possible answer.

Chapter 14

THE OTHER BEACH WAS JUST AS STEVE HAD LEFT IT the afternoon before. As he approached the crippled plane he was once again keenly aware of his helpless situation and his isolation from the rest of the world.

The late afternoon sun was still warm, and he took off his clothes and plunged into the cool surf in an effort to shock himself out of his dejection. After his dip, he ran up and down the beach to warm himself in the final rays of the setting sun.

The exercise màde him hungry again, and he dressed hurriedly. He was eager to try to make the donax soup, but first it was necessary to get the fire going.

While the wood was burning to a bed of coals he prepared the donax for cooking. To cleanse the tiny closed bivalves of sand, he rinsed them several times in sea water. When they were clean, he added fresh water to the pot and put it on the coals. As the water heated, the little shells opened, and the meat inside cooked. Soon the pot was steaming, and a savory odor rose from the contents.

When the soup was finished, he set it aside to cool while he hunted for an unbroken shell to use as a spoon. He found a long bluish-black mussel shell which would make a perfect scoop. Next he whittled a wooden pick. Using the spoon for the broth and the pick for the bits of meat from the shells, he soon emptied two-thirds of the pot. The soup was good, even better than he had expected, and the broth was not only nourishing but it satisfied his thirst. The remainder would do for breakfast, and he stored it in one of the empty bottles.

As he sat by the fire after supper Steve went over in his mind the sources of food he had already discovered. He knew that he had been lucky to find such a variety. The ocean had provided fish; the tide pools, lobsters; the cactus plants, fruit; and the beach, donax. Also, he had made two meals from Amigo's crab. If this abundance should ever diminish, he could figure out ways to snare birds, lizards, or rabbits. And he had not yet hunted for abalone, which was one of the best seafoods found on the Pacific Coast.

Food was plentiful, but water was a problem. He had only a gallon remaining from the supply he had collected at the pool. Steve knew that he could return to Amigo's pool and take more water if it had not evaporated, but meanwhile he decided to try to make a device to catch the dew. He had thought of something which might work.

It was starting to get dark, so he threw more

gasoline and wood on the fire until it burned brightly. Soon the flames were leaping high enough to light up the surrounding beach.

He made his way to the plane to get his tools. Using the pliers, screwdriver, and hammer, he worked for an hour prying off a large piece of metal from the fuselage. The piece was triangular in shape, and he bent it so that the middle formed a kind of trough. Then he placed it on a mound of dry sand, slanting it so that the triangle tip pointed downward. Underneath the trough's tip, he placed the oilcan. He had figured that the dew that collected on the metal sides would run down into the trough and, since it was slanted downward, drip into the pot. Tomorrow he would know if the device worked. If it could collect dew, he had discovered an invaluable source of water.

Steve was tired from the long day's activities, and he found himself yawning and barely able to keep his eyes open. However, before settling for the night, he walked a few yards up and down the beach calling to the coyote. He was worried about it. The wound should be treated again. He was also disappointed that his friend had not returned to camp.

"I hope the poor fellow isn't holed up someplace unable to walk," was his thought as he started for the Cessna to stretch out for the night.

As he stepped through the cabin door he heard a familiar yelp from the vicinity of the dunes. Grabbing his first-aid kit and a water bottle, he hastened to meet the coyote. It was pitch dark, but he threw more wood on the dying embers of the fire and it flared up again.

When the animal appeared in the circle of light, it was limping badly. As it caught sight of Steve it wagged its tail feebly and whined pitifully. Steve was touched. He realized that it had put forth a great deal of effort to get to him in such a state.

"Poor fellow, you're in a bad way," Steve said as he knelt down and patted the coyote's head. He felt the area around the cut. As he suspected, it was quite swollen.

"No wonder you're lame," he said as he patted the animal's head again. "You've got an infection and you'll have to let me fix it up."

The coyote obviously trusted him, so he was not afraid as he cleaned and treated the wound with sulfa powder again. He tried to coax it to drink some donax soup or some water, but it refused. It seemed exhausted and lay down on the dry sand near the fire. Steve spread his jacket over its body to keep off the dampness and went to the plane to spend the night.

In spite of his fatigue he awakened several times and listened for any distress signs from the animal. But there was no sound except the usual noise of the waves breaking on shore and the surf surging around the plane at the height of the tide.

The next morning Steve was up at daybreak. The coyote was still on the sand where he had left it. It stood up as he approached.

"You look a lot better," Steve said happily as he noticed that his jacket had given the animal some protection from the dew.

Suddenly he remembered the dew catcher. He was at the contraption in a second and on his knees.

"It worked!" he shouted as he saw the metal gleaming with moisture and drops falling into the pot. His hand shook with excitement as he picked up the container and examined the contents. He could hardly believe it, but the pot had collected about two quarts of water. Pure wonderful fresh water!

He raised the pot to his lips and drank until he could hold no more. "Nothing will ever taste so good again." He sighed as he wiped his mouth and held out the pot to the coyote. It was thirsty and lapped up a considerable amount. But Steve did not care. He had found a source of water, and he and his friend could have all they needed.

He placed the pot back under the trough to catch what moisture was still falling. The sky was getting lighter, and soon the warmth of the rising sun would evaporate the mist. He realized that he had been lucky, for the dewfall was particularly heavy that morning. There would not be such a large quantity every morning, but there would be some, and this he could store away in the bottles.

The coyote again refused the donax soup, so Steve consumed it and the two remaining cactus fruit for breakfast. As he ate he planned the day. First he would find some food, for he needed to lay in a supply. Then he would decide what to take to the other beach. He would put everything together in a pile. It would be necessary to make many trips to get the things he needed across the dunes, but it had to be done. As he thought of the labor involved in carrying everything he found himself fervently wishing that he had some kind of cart or sledge.

"Why not make a kind of travois?" he asked himself. "It should be easy."

He remembered seeing pictures of American Indians transporting their folded teepees and household goods on travois pulled by dogs or horses. He tried to recall what a travois looked like. As nearly as he could remember there were two dragging poles that served as shafts at the lifted end. A net of thongs or a wooden platform was attached between the poles at the other end, and this supported the load. It should be easy to make one if he could find pieces of wood of the proper length, and he could pull it himself with a shaft under each arm. By sliding the load over the sand dunes, he could move awkwardly shaped or particularly heavy things with a fair amount of ease.

A hasty search of the beach convinced Steve that he would have to look elsewhere for long narrow boards or slim logs to serve as shafts. He thought that it was possible he could find something suitable in the piles of driftwood which had collected at the base of the cliffs. At the same time he could search for lobsters or abalones. The tide was going out, and the tide pools would be accessible.

The sun had penetrated the morning mist and was warming the beach as he prepared to leave. He stored the water from the dew catcher in a bottle, and he carried the oilcan and a screwdriver. The screwdriver was a necessity if he happened to find abalones. They were usually firmly attached to the rocks and had to be pried loose.

Although the coyote seemed much better, it still walked with difficulty. As it showed no inclination to follow him, Steve started off alone.

Half an hour later he was climbing over the rocky area at the foot of the perpendicular cliffs, where the stacks of driftwood were piled. Currents and wave action over a period of many years had washed the floating wreckage from ships up on the rocks, where it was caught and jammed together in huge pyramids.

Steve had to move many of the top pieces to find out what was underneath. It was hard work, but he found two narrow boards that he thought would be suitable for the shafts of the travois. They were not the same length, but he figured that he could burn the end of the longer one in the fire until it was more or less even with the other. He set the wood aside to retrieve on his way back to the beach.

The tide was extremely low by the time he had located the boards, and he made his way over the rocks to the water's edge. The rocks near the water were wet and covered with seaweed, and there were deep crevices full of water between them. Steve had a hard time keeping his balance as he jumped from one slippery perch to another. He was on the lookout for abalone shells, and he peered into every deep crevice in the hopes of finding them. Finally he was rewarded for his careful search. He saw three of the mollusks attached to a ledge under a couple of feet of water. He stretched out on his stomach and reached down in the crevice to pry one loose. It was firmly attached, but by using the screwdriver as a wedge he was able to loosen it. He held it up with glee. The shell, underneath its marine growth, was a plump oval shape, greenish-black in color, and it measured over six inches in length. The animal filled the shell, but from past experience in preparing abalone, Steve knew that the big muscle in the center was the edible part.

Using the same method, he pried the other two

from the rock. They were the same size, and all three would provide him with food for several meals. After placing them in the pot, he hunted for more. He found two others as well as some two-inch-long black turbans, marine snails which were also edible.

Fresh seaweed was abundant in the area, and he made up his mind to take some back and try it. He knew that Asiatic people ate seaweed, but he had no idea which kinds or how they prepared it. He found a growth of Ulva, a light green delicate seaweed lettuce which looked edible, and he picked some and added it to the pot. Now the pot was full, and he stood up to stretch his cramped muscles.

As he did so he happened to glance seaward. There, not more than three-quarters of a mile distant, was a boat. It was a fishing boat of some kind and was passing the island slowly on its way south.

Steve shouted and waved his arms. He snatched off his shirt and waved it back and forth. He dashed madly from one slippery rock to another trying to keep parallel with the boat.

"They've just got to see me," was his frantic thought. Making a megaphone of his hands, he yelled at the top of his lungs "Help! Help!" over and over. But the boat kept on moving on its course south. 113

Finally Steve gave up. It was evident that the

helmsman was concentrating on his course. If he had looked toward the rocks, he might have seen the distant figure and the white shirt. The other men were apparently down below, or someone would have seen him.

"They'll certainly see the overturned plane as they pass the beach," Steve thought desperately as he started to run.

It took time to scramble over the wet rocks, and when he reached the plane, the boat was disappearing in the distance.

He was panting and exhausted, and he sank down on the sand to recover. He felt as if he had received a mortal blow, and unheeded tears were streaming down his cheeks.

How long he sat watching the boat fade from sight he had no idea. A cold nose thrust into his hand brought him back to reality. The coyote had lain down beside him and seemed to sense that something was wrong. As Steve patted his friend, he felt much better.

"Let's have a look at your wound, fellow," he said as he tried to swallow his bitter disappointment.

He was gratified to see that the swelling was going down. "You'll be as good as new in a day or two, Amigo, old boy," he said.

The answer was a brisk wagging of the tail.

114

Chapter 15

ALTHOUGH STEVE WAS TERRIBLY DISAPPOINTED
that the men on the fishing boat had not seen him,
he made up his mind that he would be luckier the
next time a boat passed the island. If his fire had
been burning, the smoke might have been seen.
Smoke was no guarantee that help was needed, but
at least it would attract attention.

Steve wished that he had a flare of some kind.
He began to think of ways to make a flare that
would burn slowly and throw off heavy smoke.
The match supply was getting low and it was
necessary to conserve them, but on the other hand
a smoke signal for a period each day might bring
someone to the island.

In the midst of his thoughts he suddenly remembered the pot of seafood that he had left on
the rocks in his haste to follow the boat. The tide
was rising, and it could be washed out to sea if he
did not get back quickly. The loss of his oilcan
and his jacket, which covered it, would be serious. 115
The jacket was indispensable, and the pot was useful for so many things.

When he reached the rocks where he had left the pot, he was in luck. It was still above the incoming tide. He breathed a sigh of relief as he picked up the oilcan and climbed to the place where he had set aside the boards for the travois.

It was afternoon by the time he had carried everything back. The coyote was far down the beach stalking shore birds. Steve saw a flock of birds rise in a cloud of fluttering wings as the animal dashed among them. He was pleased to see that it was limping less and that it was well enough to catch its own food.

Steve was hungry too, and he went to work preparing the abalones. He removed the meat from the shells and cut out the big center muscles with his knife. These he sliced and then tenderized by pounding them on a rock with his hammer.

When the fire had burned sufficiently, he cut the slices in pieces and placed them in the pot with some water. He added the sea lettuce and the marine snails to make a sort of stew. Then he put the pot on the coals to cook and waited to see what the concoction would taste like.

He was pleasantly surprised for the stew was appetizing and completely satisfying. He had plenty left over, and he covered the pot and surrounded it with wet sand so that the contents would keep fresh for the next day. Then he turned his attention to making a flare.

He had an idea for one, and it was important to get it working as soon as possible. He had vowed to be ready with a signal the next time a boat appeared.

While it was still broad daylight he went to the plane to get one of the bottles of oil that he had stored when he emptied the can. Next he gathered some rocks from the end of the beach and carried them back to a spot well above the tide line. He placed these in a circle and filled its center with a mound of dry sand. From the plane tank he drew several shellfuls of gas. He spread the gas over the sand mound and let it soak in, then added engine oil from the bottle. Finally he lighted a piece of newspaper from the embers of the fire and threw it in the circle. The gas flared up and ignited the oil, which produced a thick black smoke. It rose up into the sky in a dense column.

Steve was immensely pleased with the result. He figured that it would burn for a half hour or more and could easily be seen from quite a distance.

He counted his remaining matches. Although he had been extremely careful, there were only twenty left. He decided that for the present he could have only one flare a day, which he would keep going until dark. After dark, the fire was a better beacon. To save matches, he could light a stick from the flare and use it to start the fire.

Now he turned his attention to making the travois. There was still enough daylight, so he searched the beach for wood for the carrier platform and nails to fasten the wood to the shafts. He found enough nails in some of the old broken crates. They were rusty and bent, but he managed to pull them out and straighten them with his hammer so that they could be used again. These he laid aside with the wood. It was dark when he finished, and completion of the travois would have to be postponed until morning. Also, before he nailed the shafts together, he had to even them by burning the end of the longer one in the fire.

Before settling down by the fire, Steve got his clipboard from the plane. He decided that he should keep track of the days on the island and what had been accomplished. He drew a calendar on the paper, and as he recalled each day's events he wrote them down. When he had finished, he had marked off eight days, in which he had devoted nearly every minute to finding food and water, facilitating his rescue, and exploring the area. He still thought it strange that he had seen only one fishing boat in that interval of time, but it was possible that the Mexican fishing fleet was occupied elsewhere.

Since he had been lost for over a week, he wondered if the Coast Guard had given up the search for him. Occasionally fliers had been found in the

Baja wilderness after a much longer search, but Steve reminded himself that his case was different. The obvious thing for a searching party to assume was that he had plunged into the ocean during the hurricane and drowned. If this had happened, all traces of his plane could easily have been obliterated by the wind and waves.

He wondered how his family was taking the news of his disappearance. If only he had a way to give them some hope.

"I'll get to the mainland if it's the last thing I ever do," Steve promised himself. "And it might well be the last thing!" He was convinced that he would be stretching his luck to the limit if he attempted it on a raft, but if another week passed without his being rescued, he knew that he would try it.

The next morning Steve occupied himself putting the travois together. The two boards for the shafts were now even, and he laid them on the sand about three feet apart. They were approximately eight feet long. Across the ends he nailed wooden slats for a platform wide enough to carry a load.

After the travois was finished, he spent the rest of the day gathering things together for the move across the dunes to the other beach. When he had put everything in a pile, he had a sizable collection. There were twenty beach bottles of different sizes, each filled with gasoline, oil, or water; the toolbox and first-aid kit; the maps and clipboard; the oilcan containing the remains of his food; the coil of nylon rope and the spool of wire; the shovel; the metal dew collector and the fishline and hook. He added the abalone shells and some old wooden boxes that he had found in the beach debris.

Now it was time to decide what to take from the Cessna. He could always return for anything he needed, but to save frequent trips back and forth across the dunes he thought it best to strip the plane of all useful items before he established the new camp.

"I still hate to do it," he thought sadly. He could see, however, that the overturned Cessna was already a loss. The metal was encrusted with salt and beginning to corrode. The prop was broken beyond repair, and the landing gear was crooked and completely out of line.

"I'll never get her off the ground again anyway," was his unhappy thought as he opened the cabin door.

He crawled in and looked around for anything that might be of use. Since the radio was damaged beyond his ability to repair it, it was useless, but the compass and altimeter might come in handy. He removed them from the instrument panel. What else should he take?

"What about the battery?" he asked himself.

All at once it came to him that he could use it to start fires. He had wire, and he could make a direct short circuit by attaching two short strands of wire to the terminals. When the wire ends were touched together, they would create sparks.

"What an idiot I've been," he said aloud. "I could have saved myself a lot of worry if I had thought of this sooner." His only excuse was that he had been too preoccupied with food and water and his rescue.

As he took the battery out he knew that it was the answer to his dwindling match problem. He could keep several flares going at once as long as the battery lasted or until the oil gave out. Also, he would be able to have a cooking fire whenever he felt like it.

He looked around the cabin for more useful things. His eye fell on the seats and the walls. The seats were covered with plastic and the walls with a thick cotton fabric. Why not take some of both materials? He could wrap a piece of the fabric around his head for protection from sunburn and use a piece of plastic for protection from dampness. He took out his knife and ruthlessly ripped away the materials. He rolled them up and added them to the other items.

121

The next couple of hours were spent in stripping things from the outside of the plane. He removed all of the control wires and coiled them ready to go. From the fuselage he pried another piece of metal for a second dew collector, and he removed the cowlings from the engine. Lastly he took off one of the wheels and added it to the pile. He did not know exactly what he intended to do with all these things, but he thought that he might need some of them for the raft.

The day had passed swiftly while he worked, but by nightfall he had everything ready to transport. Although he had not seen a single ship during the day, he was in better spirits than he had been the day before.

He tried out the battery and succeeded in igniting a gasoline-soaked stick with the sparks. It was cheering to think that he was no longer dependent on matches.

That night he examined the coyote again and was glad to find that its wound was healing nicely. Amigo would be able to go with him the next morning when he started moving.

Chapter 16

||||||||||||||||||||||||||||||||||||||||||||||||||||||||||||||||||||||||||||||||||||

THE NEXT THREE DAYS WERE FULL OF HARD WORK.
Steve spent the mornings moving things across the
dunes and the afternoons setting up camp and
obtaining food. The coyote was with him most
of the time, but its wound had almost healed, and
it went off alone for a period each night. Steve
assumed that it was hunting for birds or mice.
It did not seem hungry when he offered it cooked
fish or donax soup, and he supposed that it pre-
ferred its regular diet.

As time passed, Steve became certain that the
coyote was the only one of its kind on the island.
He had not seen nor heard another, and the island
was small enough so that if there had been others
they would have been attracted long ago to his
camp. He still held to his theory that Amigo had
been raised on the mainland by a Mexican fisherman and had been left on the island at some time
or other. It was the only possible explanation.

The travois proved to be a big help in shifting
his things from one beach to another. He was able
to drag the bulky airplane parts by roping them on

the wooden platform and sliding them over the slippery dunes. To protect his arms from the rough ends of the shafts as he pulled the travois along, he had wrapped them with fabric from the interior of the plane.

By the second afternoon Steve had completed a crude shelter, which he set up on the dry sand facing the ocean. It was made of pieces of driftwood that he had found on the beach. He had fitted them together as closely as possible and anchored them upright in holes in the sand. There were many gaps in the three-sided wall when he had finished, but he filled them with other pieces of wood to make the shelter more or less windproof. It was impractical to try to anchor a roof on the top, as the walls were too short and uneven, but the shelter was partial protection from blowing sand and the afternoon sun. To avoid being soaked by the dewfall at night, Steve covered himself with the plastic material from the Cessna's seats.

One of the first things that he set up in the new camp were the two pieces of metal for collecting dew. He had scrubbed out two of the big turtle shells left by the former campers and used them as receptacles to catch the dripping moisture. This left the oilcan pot free for cooking and collecting food.

He built his fire now in a pit made of rocks.

These he had hauled from the end of the beach. He had placed the fire pit directly in front of his three-sided shelter, and at night he could sit inside and still feel the fire's warmth. Every day since he had thought of using the plane's battery he had been successful in starting the fire and in lighting two gasoline and oil-soaked sand flares, which he burned at intervals during the daylight hours. This left the matches for emergencies or for use elsewhere on the island.

He had also set up two other devices for attracting attention from any passing boats. They were the metal cowlings that had covered the plane engine. By rubbing coarse sand repeatedly over the inside of the metal, he had polished it so that it reflected the sun's rays.

Food was as readily available at the new camp as it was at the old. The donax were plentiful, and fish rose to his bait when Steve threw out his line. He had made a grill of woven wire, which covered the fire pit, and he broiled the fish on it. The fish and donax were adequate for survival while he was setting up camp, but his body craved a more varied diet. He planned to hunt for more cactus fruit and sea lettuce, as well as lobsters and crabs, as soon as the camp was set up.

On the third and last day of moving, when Steve returned to the plane for the final load, he placed pieces of driftwood up on the dry sand in the shape of a large arrow. It pointed across the dunes to the new camp. In the event that anyone came ashore, the wrecked plane and the arrow would tell the story.

Before he roped the plane wheel on the travois, he took a last look around to be sure that he had everything he wanted. As he searched the area around the plane he came across a bottle that apparently had washed ashore since he had last been on the beach. The surf had carried it beyond the plane, and it had washed back and was stuck behind the fuselage.

Steve picked it up and examined it. It was a narrow bottle about eight inches long and was tightly capped. He could see that there was a piece of paper inside. He removed the plastic cover and tight cork with his knife and took out the rolled paper. It was a printed form card and on it was a message in English and another in Spanish He read:

NOTICE TO FINDER

These cards are being used to study the currents of the Pacific Ocean. Please fill in the blank spaces. Mail every card you find. No postage needed in U.S. In return you will be told time and place of their release. Thank you.

Steve noted that the same notice was also in Spanish and that there were spaces for the finder's name and address, the hour found, and the exact location. When he turned it over he saw that the card was addressed to the University of California's Scripps Institution of Oceanography, which was located near San Diego.

As he examined the card Steve felt a deep pang of nostalgia. The message was a link with home, and his pent-up homesickness suddenly engulfed him.

"I'm going to get off this island some way!" he said with conviction.

His luck had held out so far, for he had survived the crash, he had found food and water, and although he was much thinner, he was still in good physical shape. Now he knew it was up to him to get back to civilization before his luck ran out. He had marked the eleventh day on his calendar that morning. He would allow himself a few more days of waiting for rescue, and then he would build the raft and try to make it alone.

As he tucked the card in his pocket Steve had a thought. "Why not send a message myself?" The cork was broken but it might keep out water for a few days. He could weight the bottle with sand to keep it fairly upright. It was unlikely that anything would ever come of his message but there was the possibility that the bottle might wash ashore on the mainland and alert someone of his predicament.

When he reached the camp with his last load, Steve saw the coyote curled up in the shelter. He was delighted that his friend had accepted the new location and seemed to want to stay with him.

Steve was tired from his trip, and he dropped down in his shelter for a much needed rest. He had made his bed along the back wall of the shelter with quantities of dried eelgrass spread on the sand. On this he had placed some of the pieces of fabric from the plane.

While he rested Steve surveyed his handiwork. He had stored all of his possessions in the old crates that he had brought from the other beach. One served as a cupboard for the battery and the bottles of gas, oil, and water; and in another he had stored his maps, clipboard, toolbox, and medicine kit. Two smaller boxes held his food and small items such as his pen and pencil, wallet, the rest of the newspaper, the two magazines, the one remaining candy bar, which he had kept for an emergency, and his matches. He had rolled the Cessna's altimeter and compass in a piece of plastic to protect them in case he would need them in the future. Everything had to be protected from the dampness in the night.

The shelter proved to be a good windbreak.

Until the weather turned colder or it rained, it would be adequate protection. The days were now overcast for long periods, but it was still the tag end of summer.

After his rest, Steve got his pen and a piece of paper from the clipboard. He started to write a message for the bottle when he remembered that he could not describe exactly where he was. The only information that he could convey was that he was on an island approximately fifty miles off the coast of Baja California, probably somewhere between Turtle Bay and San Ignacio Lagoon.

"After all," he thought, "this island is isolated from the others, and its existence must be known to some of the Mexicans living near the coast." In any event he was not losing anything by sending the message.

When he had finished, he had printed the following information:

SEPTEMBER 7

S O S

MY PLANE CRASHED ON THIS ISLAND ELEVEN DAYS AGO. I AM STRANDED HERE. WILL THE FINDER OF THIS MESSAGE PLEASE SEND A BOAT FOR ME AS SOON AS POSSIBLE OR NOTIFY U.S. COAST GUARD IMMEDIATELY. THE ISLAND IS 40 OR 50 MILES FROM THE COAST OF BAJA CALIFORNIA. PROBABLY OPPOSITE THE AREA

BETWEEN TURTLE BAY AND SAN IGNACIO LA-
GOON. I AM CAMPED ON THE SMALL BEACH
ON THE EAST SIDE OF THE ISLAND. ALL EX-
PENSES FOR MY RESCUE WILL BE REIMBURSED.
STEVE FERRIS
2540 FIRST ST.
SAN DIEGO, CALIFORNIA, U.S.A.

With his very limited knowledge of Spanish, he could not translate the message, but he thought a long time and then added:

S O S   S O S
ACCIDENTE AEROPLANO EN LA ISLA PROXIMA
LA COSTA DE BAJA CALIFORNIA ENTRE BAHIA
TORTUGAS Y LAGUNA SAN IGNACIO! SE LLAMA
STEVE FERRIS. VIVO 2540 FIRST ST., SAN
DIEGO, CALIFORNIA, ESTADOS UNIDOS.
S O S   S O S   S O S   S O S

After he had finished printing the message, Steve put some sand in the bottom of the bottle and placed the rolled-up paper inside. He could see that the cork was not going to prevent water from entering the bottle, so he looked around for something to use as a seal. His eye fell on the plane tire. If he wrapped a piece of rubber from the inner tube around the cork, it might help.

He got his tools and pried the tire off the wheel.

With his knife he cut a small piece of rubber from the tube. This he wrapped in several thicknesses around the cork and then stoppered the bottle.

"Tomorrow," he decided, "I'll launch it from the south end of the island." He had already made plans to explore that section anyway. There it might catch in a current that would keep it from floating back to the beach. He had no hope that the message would ever be found, but he was desperate enough to try anything.

Chapter 17

IT WAS COLD AND WINDY THE NEXT MORNING WHEN Steve crawled out of his shelter to start the fire. During the night a thick layer of sand had drifted all over his fire pit. It took him a while to dig it out, lay fresh wood, and get the fire burning.

It was low tide, and while the fire burned to a bed of coals he gathered enough donax for a pot of soup. He needed a hearty breakfast to carry him through the day, which he planned to devote exploring the island's south tip.

As soon as he had satisfied his appetite, Steve made preparations to leave camp for the day. He lighted the flares, which were placed along the beach. To keep them burning longer he added some pieces of the plane upholstery soaked with oil, as well as some pieces of the rubber inner tube. The smoldering material and rubber created a much blacker smoke than the oil and gas alone.

"If a boat comes near, the crew can't miss this signal," he observed as he watched the black smoke rise in columns. Then the wind caught it and carried it out over the water where it was soon diffused in the overcast.

Steve was disappointed that the smoke was not more concentrated, but he had done all he could for the present. If the overcast lifted soon, the smoke could be easily seen from a distance of four or five miles.

As a last precaution, in case he missed someone landing on the beach, he laid wood in the shape of an arrow pointing in the direction he was to go.

It was the middle of the morning by the time Steve was ready to leave. He took the oilcan, a bottle of water, some matches, and his knife, as well as the bottle containing the message. He wore his jacket, for he remembered that he had regretted not having it on his other exploratory trip. Around his head he had wrapped a piece of fabric for protection from wind and sun.

As he started off he called to the coyote. It knew its way around the island, and also he had learned to depend upon it for companionship. It bounded off ahead, as Steve made his way to the end of the beach.

When he reached the top of the low cliff, Steve glanced back to see how the flares were doing. They were still throwing off dense smoke, which merged into a cloud over the water. It was not what he had intended, but it could not be helped.

Steve figured that it was about two miles to the end of the island. The cliffs were lower and less rugged than those he had traversed on the other side, and he made pretty good time for about a mile and a half. He kept scanning the ocean as he walked along, but the overcast was too thick for him to see more than a mile offshore. If there were any boats beyond, they were screened by the cloud cover.

As he neared the end of the island, he began to see great numbers of sea birds. Flocks of cormorants, stretching their long necks, rose in consternation; and several ospreys hovered overhead as he passed along the edge of the cliff. He was curious to see where they came from, and he got down on his hands and knees and looked over the rim of the cliff. Along the sheer face of the cliff were eroded holes and ledges which served as perches for the birds. Steve knew nothing about the habits of cormorants, but he imagined that this was the rookery where the young were hatched in spring. The cliff ledges were well suited for the nesting habits of sea birds. Fish were easily obtainable for food, and the nests were well protected. Even the sure-footed coyote would not venture to climb down the cliff wall.

As he stood up to continue Steve decided that this was as good a place as he would be likely to find for launching his bottle. The distance from the top of the cliff to the water was perhaps thirty feet, and the water surging around the base looked deep and devoid of rocks.

Removing the bottle from his pocket, he gave it a mighty fling, arching it as far out over the water as possible. It landed some distance from the cliffs and was immediately caught in the swells. As it hit the water, several ospreys which had been hovering overhead swooped down after it.

"Leave it alone, you crazy birds," Steve shouted. But in spite of his shouts and the coyote's excited yelps one bird dove with outstretched claws and soared upward with the bottle in its grasp.

"Drop it," Steve shouted. He knew that if the bird flew off with the bottle it would soon break it on a rock. He had seen gulls drop closed shells on rocks to break them so that they could get at the meat.

As he watched the bird circled out to sea to avoid its competitors. Either the bottle proved to be too heavy or the bird realized that it had no food inside, for in a minute Steve saw the bottle drop back into the water. The osprey made no attempt to retrieve it but flew back to the cliff, where it joined the cormorants in a noisy tirade of harsh throaty cries.

Steve watched the bottle eagerly as it rode up and down the swells. Finally it seemed to be caught in a current which propelled it seaward.

"Well, that's that." He sighed. "Now we'll see if anything comes of it."

Actually, he thought, the bird had bettered the bottle's chances of floating away from the island by carrying it farther out.

After watching the birds a few minutes longer,

Steve continued along the top of the cliff. The coyote had gone ahead and was out of sight.

Before long Steve reached his destination, the rounded rocky tip of the island. As far as he could see there was nothing, only the gray ocean reflecting the gray sky. There was no land in sight, and there were no boats of any kind. It was disappointing, but it was about what he had expected. The weather was still too overcast to see ships from any distance anyway.

All around where Steve stood the rocks were covered with bird droppings, and several different kinds of sea birds were scattered over the area. They were making so much noise that he could hardly hear the waves breaking on the rocks. The birds rose in protesting clouds of fluttering wings as he walked into their domain.

Steve wished that he could find a clutch of eggs, and he searched for one, but the search was fruitless. He concluded that the birds must only nest in spring. It was too bad; he had heard that the eggs of some sea birds were very good to eat.

He looked around for the coyote, but because of its tawny color, which blended so well with the landscape, it was often hard to spot. Finally he saw it out on the brown seaweed-covered rocks at the water's edge. It was watching some sea lions in the ocean about fifty yards from shore. Their heads were bobbing up and down in the waves, and they were either playing or diving for fish.

Steve joined the coyote. He intended to look for abalones and lobsters, and off the rocks was a good place. Putting the water bottle and the oilcan in a safe spot, he removed his clothes and slipped off the eelgrass-covered rocks into the water.

The tide was not high, but the water was quite deep. He had to swim fast to keep from being dashed back against the rocks as the water surged in and out. He swam parallel to the rocky shore, looking in crevices for abalones and lobsters.

Not far from where he had entered the water he discovered the opening to a watery cave which extended far back under a ledge. He swam to the entrance and peered in. It was semi-dark, and the walls dripped with moisture from the ocean spray. It was an excellent place to hunt for abalones, and Steve swam in without any hesitation. He expected that there would be moray eels hidden among the rocks under the water, but he intended taking the chance of encountering one.

As he had expected, the abalones were plentiful. He grabbed at one quickly before it had time to get a tight grip on the cave wall. Then he captured two others. These were smaller than the one he had found previously and were green in color. He gripped all three tightly as he propelled himself backward out of the cave with his feet.

It was difficult swimming with the mollusks in

137

his hand, and this slowed his approach to the rock where he had left his clothes. As he neared it, he saw a sleek brown head in the water a few yards away. At first he thought it was Amigo, but then he realized that it was a sea lion and that it was coming toward him.

He was not exactly afraid, but he had a feeling that the seal was after the abalones and might try to snatch one from his hand. He had heard that sea lions sometimes appeared when skin divers were spearing fish and in one instance had taken the fish from the spear before the diver could get ashore with it.

Steve quickened his pace and fortunately reached the rock ahead of the seal. He threw the abalones up on the rock and pulled himself up on the slippery eelgrass just as the seal caught up with him.

Its small, whiskered face and limpid brown eyes looked so innocent that Steve was sure that he had mistaken its intention. It was probably merely curious. Soon it disappeared under the water and joined its comrades, who were still swimming in and out of the waves farther offshore.

Steve was glad to see the seal leave. He had no intention of parting with his abalones. They were 138 fine specimens and would furnish him meat for several good meals.

After he dressed, he put the abalones in the oilcan and covered them with wet seaweed to keep them fresh. It was already early afternoon, and he still wanted to climb the low hill which rose inland from the coast, so he started off at a brisk pace.

The ascent up the hill was fairly easy, for the elevation was much lower than that of the hill at the north end. The slopes were similarly dotted with low shrubs and cactus plants.

Steve was delighted to find more stands of prickly pear, and he knocked off some of the fruit to take back to camp. He also found some plants with buds and lobes which had not yet developed spines or prickly needles. He remembered that someone had once told him that the aboriginal Indians of Baja had cooked the cactus plant lobes and eaten them, and he asked himself, "Why not try them?"

He picked up as many as he could take in the pot along with the fruit and abalones. It was getting late when he had finished, and he started back to camp in the late afternoon.

It was six o'clock when he finally got to the beach. Amigo had preceded him and greeted him with a happy bark.

The beach was now warm and dry, for in the late afternoon the sun had finally penetrated the overcast. The flares had burned out, but Steve soon had a roaring fire going in the fire pit. He was extremely hungry, and he went to work preparing the abalones and the cactus for cooking.

He had no idea how to best cook the cactus lobes and buds, but he decided to cut them into strips similar to string beans. They were not too tough, and after boiling them in water for a considerable length of time, they seemed tender enough to eat.

"Now I'll see whether cactus is edible or not," he said as he picked up one of the string-bean-like strips and chewed it.

"Not bad," he decided as he experimented with another piece. The flavor was reminiscent of artichoke and the texture somewhat like okra.

Steve was quite pleased with his find. When he had finished some of the abalone and a portion of the cactus, he ate two of the sweet cactus fruits for dessert. For the first time since he had landed on the island, he felt that he had had a fairly balanced and satisfying meal.

Chapter 18

THE NEXT MORNING STEVE MARKED THE FOUR-
teenth day on his calendar. He could hardly believe that it had been two weeks since he had seen
another human being. He decided to allow himself
one more day to explore the island before beginning the task of making a raft. He had not seen the
extreme northern end, and he still hoped to find
some more evidence that the island had been occupied. He was even optimistic enough to think
that it was possible that a boat might be anchored
offshore at the other end.

After lighting the flares, he filled a bottle with
water from the dew collector and wrapped some
abalone meat in paper and dropped it in his
pocket. He knew that it was a longer trip to the
north end, probably three and a half or four miles,
but the round trip could easily be made during the
daylight hours.

When he left the beach and started to climb to
the top of the cliffs, the coyote joined him. It had
been stalking shore birds, but it seemed to prefer
to go along with Steve.

Steve found the walking much more difficult along the north coast. The high hill that he had climbed to get his overall view of the island rose abruptly inland from this side. To avoid creating a landslide, which could send him tumbling over the cliffs into the ocean, he had to pick his way carefully along the steep slope.

It was three hours before he glimpsed the rocky end of the island jutting out into the sea. Separated from the point were several high exposed rocks which at one time had probably been part of the headland. Storm waves, pounding at the point over many years, had eaten away the connecting land, and now the rocks were miniature islands.

As Steve approached the point he could just make out a number of seals sunning themselves on the flat top of the largest rock, which was about a hundred yards offshore. But there were no boats anchored anywhere in the vicinity.

Steve swallowed his disappointment as he drew nearer to watch the seals. He had not really expected to see a boat, but he had convinced himself that there was a possibility.

When he was close enough to get a good look at the seals, he stared in surprise. The animals on the rock were not the usual California sea lions but were much bigger and heavier. A few of them appeared to be about fifteen feet long with great massive bodies.

The tide was quite low, and Steve removed his shoes and slacks and waded out to get a closer view. He moved cautiously, for he was afraid of frightening the huge mammals into the water before he had a good look at them. He pulled himself up on a small rock halfway between the shore and the seals. Lowering himself flat on the top, he turned to watch, fascinated at the scene before him.

There were perhaps two dozen of the gargantuan creatures. Some were asleep, and others were moving their massive heads around, alerted by his presence. Several smaller animals, probably youngsters, were moving about among the adults. Some had huge protruding noses, which gave them a strange comic look. Steve knew it was this distinguishing feature that gave them their name, elephant seal or sea elephant.

Steve realized that he was witnessing an unusual sight. He had once read an article on the history of the elephant seal in Baja California. He recalled that the author had stated that the strange mammals were formerly abundant in the Antarctic and off the coast of Baja but that predacious hunters had almost wiped the herds out. This wanton slaughter was responsible for a Mexican law which now made it illegal to kill them. According to the article, the herds had built up again but were found only on a few uninhabited islands far from the coast.

Steve remained motionless on the rock, but he

could see that the seals were becoming restive. Those asleep had wakened, and others were roaring loudly. They were starting to move about with their awkward flippers, and some had lunged off the rock into the water.

Suddenly the commotion increased, and those left on the rock began roaring at the swimmers. Steve wondered what was making them so nervous since he himself had made no move toward them. Soon he saw the cause of their alarm.

A black triangular fin was cutting through the water at great speed toward the swimming seals. Steve was horrified when he realized that it must be a killer whale. It was the one natural enemy of the elephant seal and a menace to every other mammal in the sea.

Steve was tingling with excitement as he saw the swimmers moving frantically toward the rock. He found himself yelling to the seals, "Hurry up!" One by one they lunged up on a shelf at the base of the rock to join those on top. Finally they were all safe but one of the youngsters, who was still quite far from the rock.

As the black fin came closer to the swimming seal, Steve shouted at the top of his lungs. He thrashed his arms back and forth, hoping in some way to attract the killer whale's attention and divert it. But on it came, straight for the helpless young seal, who was not able to swim fast enough to make the rock in time. Steve could see the top of the monster's great long body above the water and its open mouth filled with long pointed teeth. It looked to be twenty-five or thirty feet long.

Just as Steve resigned himself to the seal's fate, he saw the monster suddenly change course and veer away. It seemed to be struggling to free itself from a shoal. Steve realized with glee that it had run aground in too shallow water. While it churned the water in an attempt to free itself from the shoal, the young seal reached the rock unscathed and lunged out onto the rock shelf. At that moment the killer whale freed itself, but it was too late. The seal had joined the others at the top of the rock, where the whole group were still roaring in a thunderous chorus. The frustrated monster circled the rock, then headed back out to sea.

It had been a dramatic moment, and Steve breathed a sigh of relief when it was over. He was glad that he had been a witness to the killer whale's frustration. It was the most rapacious murderer in the sea and preyed particularly on the harmless California gray whale.

While he had been intent on the scene, it had not occurred to him to worry about his own safety. However, now that the villain had departed, he felt weak when he recalled its mouth full of sharp teeth. He was ignorant of the habits of killer whales, but he knew that they were considered even more dangerous than sharks. Surfers and divers always made a hasty exit to the beach if the monsters were anywhere in the vicinity.

Steve glanced at his watch. It was two o'clock and high time he started back to camp if he were to make it before night. Also, the tide had risen while he was perched on the rock, and the water was getting deeper between the rock and shore.

He stood up from his cramped position to stretch. His legs were somewhat numb from immobility, and as he stepped into a crevice in the rock his foot caught. He wrenched his ankle so severely that it caused him to lose his balance and fall back on the rock.

The pain was almost unbearable, and he broke into a sweat and felt faint and nauseated. He closed his eyes and lay prone. Pains were shooting up and down his leg, and it was all he could do to keep from blacking out.

After a few minutes the intense pain subsided enough for him to sit up and examine his foot. The ankle was starting to swell and turn blue. He knew that he had either broken it or sprained it badly.

"Now what do I do?" Steve thought disgustedly and with considerable alarm. He was several miles from camp and stuck on a rock in the middle of water that was rising rapidly. The longer he stayed on the rock, the more difficult it would be to get back to where he had left his shoes, slacks, and water bottle.

He felt his ankle again. It was already swollen to twice its normal size and was extremely tender to touch. He knew that he should not put his weight on it, and he began to feel panicky.

"What a stupid thing to do," he said to himself with disgust. His survival was entirely dependent on his physical well-being, and now his chances were jeopardized. But the immediate problem was to get to shore, then he would plan how best to get himself back to camp.

He stood up and tried to balance on his good foot using the injured foot to steady himself, but when he put any weight on the ankle he felt faint again. If the bone was broken, he should not try to walk. However, he could not stay on the rock.

"Well, here goes," he said aloud. He gritted his teeth and slid off the rock into the water expecting to touch bottom. The tide, however, had risen more than he realized, and he had to start swimming. It was now a longer distance to the dry rocks, and he was handicapped in the water by his jacket.

Finally he made it, and as he waded ashore he tried to keep the weight off his ankle. The cold water had numbed it somewhat, but he was afraid of risking further injury. He had to hop and pull himself from one slippery rock to another until he reached the dry rocks where he had left his things.

147

He sat down to recover and to wring out his

jacket, which was soaked. His foot was very swollen and discolored and looked unnatural.

"I should bind it with something," he decided as he felt the tender flesh, "but what can I use?"

He had left his tee shirt in camp and his undershorts were the only possibility. They could be torn into strips. They were still wet from his swim, but he took them off and spread them to dry with his jacket. It was not yet three o'clock, and the sun was still warm.

As Steve pulled his slacks on over his injured foot he was forced to face the fact that he could never make it back to the beach before night. He would have to walk at a snail's pace to protect his ankle, and it would be dark long before he reached the beach. Walking after dark was out of the question, for he might stumble or trip and injure himself further.

He concluded that he would have to spend the night someplace along the way. The idea was not appealing. He had no food left and very little water; he had drunk thirstily after his exertions in getting ashore.

As he waited for his things to dry he looked around for the coyote. It had been with him when he waded out to watch the seals, but in the ensuing excitement he had forgotten about it. He assumed that it must have returned to camp.

By five o'clock the undershorts were dry enough to tear into bandages. He bound the ankle as best he could with strips of cloth and secured them with smaller strips. He knew that if the bone was broken he would have to make some kind of splint when he reached camp. From then on he didn't know what would happen, but he decided not to dwell on the future.

When he tried to put on his shoes, he found that he could wear only one. It was impossible to get the other over the thick wad of bandages, so he tied it around his neck with the laces. His jacket was almost dry, and he put it on as he got to his feet.

Now it was time to start the ordeal. He had many more rocks to cross before he came to firm ground, and he dreaded it. The binding helped some, but a stab of pain shot through his ankle every time he was forced to balance himself.

He wiped the sweat from his brow and sighed with relief as he finally crossed the last rocks and stood on even ground. Now he had to make his way along the cliff top until he came to the steep slope of the hill. He planned to keep on until complete exhaustion or darkness overtook him. Then he would just stop and lie down for the night. He remembered seeing a rock formation that morning that was not too far and might be a possibility for shelter.

It was an hour or more before he saw the place he had in mind. He had been limping along slowly and favoring his ankle, but as it was beginning to hurt with a vengeance, he was relieved to see the group of rocks ahead. A thicket of shrubs grew around them, and the place looked protected.

Steve examined it carefully. Underneath an overhanging ledge, he discovered an opening. He got down on his hands and knees and looked in. It was a perfect retreat, protected from the wind and snug and dry. He crawled in, thankful to be off his feet at last.

It was not yet dark, and after Steve had settled his ankle in a comfortable position and satisfied his thirst with the remaining water in his bottle, he examined his rocky cavern. He saw that some animal had been there before him. There were a number of bird and rodent bones as well as tufts of matted hair strewn about. Steve was puzzled. He had not seen evidence of the presence of any large animals on the island, and he was convinced that there were no coyotes other than Amigo.

Suddenly it dawned on him. The animal using the lair must have been Amigo. This was undoubtedly where the coyote had slept and had holed up during bad weather. Since it had been with him for the last week and a half, he did not think it had used the cave recently. He wondered if Amigo was at the camp now awaiting his return.

Before long Steve's eyes closed. He was weak, hungry, and exhausted from the day's misadventure, and he soon drifted off to sleep.

Chapter 19

THE CAVERN, ALTHOUGH PROTECTED, WAS FAR FROM comfortable, and Steve found himself waking up at intervals during the night. His ankle throbbed, and it was difficult to rest it properly on the hard-packed dirt that formed the cavern floor.

Sometime in the middle of the night, when he had awakened cold and uncomfortable for the fourth or fifth time, he heard a familiar whine outside the cave opening. Soon a furry body crawled in next to him. Although it was pitch dark, he knew that it was Amigo. He reached out his hand and patted the animal, who in turn licked his hand.

"Welcome home, Amigo," Steve said affectionately.

The presence of the coyote was cheering, and with the warmth of its body next to him, Steve soon fell asleep again.

When he next opened his eyes, a murky daylight was just penetrating under the ledge. He glanced at the luminous dial of his watch. It was after six and time to get going if he hoped to make the beach in good time that day. He felt weak from hunger and thirst, and his ankle still throbbed, but it was absolutely essential to get back to camp as soon as he could.

As Steve sat up and rubbed his ankle, the coyote stood up and stretched. It followed him as he crawled out of the cave.

"Now we'll see about this old ankle," Steve said as he tested his weight on the injured foot. It was still extremely painful, and he drew his foot up quickly.

"Well, it's certain that I can't put much pressure on that foot," he concluded. "I'll have to find something to use as a cane."

He started looking among the shrubs growing around the cave. Finally he spotted what he was looking for. It was a bush with long branches growing close to the ground, and they seemed thick enough to partially support his weight.

He eased himself carefully down by the bush. After choosing a particularly sturdy branch, he took out his knife and opened the largest blade. It was quite a task to cut the branch with his knife, and an hour passed before he had removed it from the bush and trimmed it to suit his purpose.

When he tried it out, he was gratified to see that it would be adequate and would enable him to travel a little faster. Calling to the coyote, he started back along the way he had come the day before.

Before long Steve's empty stomach began nagging him, but his hunger pangs were minor compared to his thirst. The effort he was expending in hobbling along made him thirstier than he would have been under normal circumstances. His mouth and throat felt parched.

He stopped to lick the morning dew from some rocks, but there was too little of it to give him any relief. He was disgusted with himself for having used up all of the water in the bottle the previous day. There was plenty of water in camp, but it would be hours before he could get to it at the slow rate he was forced to travel.

His ankle began bothering him again, and he decided to rest awhile and elevate his foot. He removed the bandages and examined the distorted ankle. It was still swollen and discolored and tender to the touch. He saw that it was going to be necessary to keep off it for several days when he reached camp. He could not tell if the bone was broken until the swelling subsided, and it was better not to try to walk on it until he knew. He rewrapped the ankle and bemoaned his bad luck.

As he started to rise he happened to notice a cactus plant growing nearby. It was a small barrel-shaped plant covered with tough spines. Steve had seen a number of them on the island, but he had paid little attention to them. This time as he looked at the plant his mind suddenly clicked. 153

"There's water inside that cactus," he said. Many a thirsty man on the desert had been revived by drinking the liquid from the barrel cactus, and Steve wondered why he had not thought of it before.

He got up and limping over to the plant knocked it over with his stick. Then, kneeling down, he cut off the top with his knife. Inside the plant was soft and pulpy with juice. The problem facing him was how to concentrate the liquid so that he could drink it. He studied the plant. Finally he decided to scoop out some of the center of the plant to form a kind of basin. Then, setting the plant upright again, he mashed the pulp around the hollow with his stick. As he had thought, this forced the liquid into the hollow, where he could scoop it up with his hands. He drank eagerly. The liquid was almost tasteless and quite palatable. It was as thirst-quenching as a glass of water, and Steve felt much better able to continue on his way.

It was early afternoon when he finally hobbled across the beach and thankfully dropped down on his bed in the shelter. He was faint from hunger, but he was so exhausted from the long painful journey that it was half an hour before he had strength enough to rise and get out his store of food. Fortunately, he had plenty of abalone meat left, as well as some cactus lobes and fruit, for he was in no condition to hobble down to the water to try to catch a fish.

When he felt stronger, he unbound his ankle.

It had not improved, and if anything even looked worse. He soaked some of the strips of cloth in water and applied them to the swollen flesh. Later, when he felt able to walk down to the ocean, he could immerse his foot in the cool surf to help reduce the swelling.

While he lay recovering from his ordeal, Steve realized that he had to revise the plans he had made for the next few days. He would have to give up building the raft until his ankle was better. It was absolutely necessary to stay off his foot until he knew whether the bone had been broken. This was impossible to tell until the swelling subsided, and he could experiment with moving the joint. If he found a broken bone, his only recourse was to bind it with a splint of some kind and wait for it to heal. How long that would be he could not tell, but in the meantime someone might come to his rescue.

As he mused over his dilemma, Steve was grateful that, other than his injured ankle, he was in pretty good physical shape. He had lost a number of pounds, and his skin was dark and leathery from constant exposure, but he was healthy.

He felt his shaggy, matted hair, and he was glad that he could not see himself in a mirror. In fifteen days his beard had grown considerably, and it was equally unkempt.

Although he had washed his clothes several times in the ocean, they were stained with oil, charcoal, and smoke from the fire. It was impossible to get them clean without soap. His cotton slacks were ripped in a couple of places, and, since he had torn up his shorts for bandages, he had no underwear. The nylon jacket, in spite of its soaking the day before, still looked all right. And the tee shirt, although full of holes, was still wearable. He had long ago discarded his worn socks, but his shoes were still in good shape.

After taking stock of himself, Steve had no doubt that he looked like a real castaway.

Since he was forced to remain in camp until his ankle at least partially healed, Steve made up his mind to do what he could toward preparing some food for the raft in case it turned out to be his only means of getting to the mainland. He reasoned that the raft might drift around for two or three days before reaching land, and he would need rations aboard. Fresh fish spoiled rapidly, and he decided to experiment with drying some while he was confined to camp.

The accident to his ankle had been most unfortunate, but the enforced idleness would also give him a chance to plan the raft before he started collecting the wood on the other side and dragging it across the dunes.

156   In the meantime there was always the chance that a boat would pass the island and that his smoke signals would be seen.

Chapter 20

||||||||||||||||||||||||||||||||||||||||||||||||||||||||||||||||||||||||||||||||||||||||||||||||||||||||||||||

THE NEXT FEW DAYS WERE MORE DIFFICULT IN A
way than any Steve had so far experienced on the
island. The inactivity that he imposed upon himself in order to save his ankle from further strain
was very frustrating. Although the days were
mostly overcast, he found himself gazing out to
sea for long intervals, hoping against hope to see
some sign of a boat. As time passed and no means
of rescue appeared, he had to curb his eagerness
to get started hauling wood for the raft.

To aid himself in walking from the shelter to
the water, he had made a pair of crude crutches.
First he had removed a couple of narrow boards
from the shelter framework, then on top of each
he had nailed a crosspiece of wood to fit under his
arm. These he padded with rubber from the
inner tube to protect his underarms. Other cross-
pieces, nailed lower down on the boards, served as
handholds. The crutches were primitive, but they
helped him to keep his injured foot elevated when
he went to the water to fish or combed the area
for firewood. To aid in carrying wood back to the
fire he had made a sling of the plane fabric which

157

he hoisted over his back and tied around his head.

As the days passed the swelling in the ankle decreased, and it was with infinite relief that Steve came to the conclusion that no bones were broken. It was just a very severe sprain, and the wrench could have torn some of the ligaments, which would account for the delay in healing. Each day he soaked the injured foot alternately in warm sea water, which he heated over the fire, and then in the cold surf when he bathed or fished.

Since he had plenty of time on his hands, he was gradually amassing a store of dried fish. By trial and error, he was soon quite expert at drying them. To prepare the fish, he cut them in strips or split them down the back, then threaded them on a stick which he suspended above the fire. When the moisture was removed from the flesh, there was no danger of spoilage.

Also while confined to the beach, Steve improvised several useful items. He made small camp lights out of the rusty tin cans left on the beach by the turtle fishermen. He used strips of the plane fabric for wicks and filled the cans with gas- and oil-soaked sand. These he kept burning for a period every night. They made the camp more cheerful and illuminated a larger area than was possible with the fire alone.

By the third day of his restricted activity, Steve found that his gasoline and oil supply was nearly out and that he would have to discontinue the big smoke flares which he had kept going at intervals daily. He could get more gas from the plane tanks, but that would have to be postponed until he was able to use his ankle normally.

The morning that he marked the twentieth day on the calendar, his morale was at a low ebb. His ankle had definitely improved, but it was still weak, and as yet he was afraid to put all his weight on it. He was sick of his diet of fish and donax, and contributing to his depression was the fact that neither the flares nor the fires had attracted anyone to the island. The overcast gave him the continual feeling that he was isolated from the rest of the world.

At night, he thought of home constantly. He tried to imagine what his family and Barbara must be feeling when no trace of him had ever been found. They must certainly have given him up for dead. Sometimes, sitting in front of the fire, he would concentrate so hard on the faces of his loved ones that he felt that they must know that he was still alive and thinking of them. If it had not been for Amigo's presence, he knew that he would have been even more depressed and discouraged.

When he had finished marking the calendar, he made a decision. "Tomorrow it will be three weeks since I landed on this place, and I'm going to get off as soon as it's humanly possible."

He spent the remainder of the day exercising his weak ankle and trying to strengthen it. He walked back and forth on firm sand as much as he could stand at a time. By evening he had made some progress and was able to walk slowly along the length of the beach without the crutches or stick. With a tight binding on his ankle the next day, he felt it might be possible to cross the dunes to the plane.

That night Steve sat by the fire longer than usual. His thoughts were filled with plans for making the raft, and he was in a more cheerful mood. The weather was partly responsible. The overcast had cleared, and it was the first evening in a week that the stars were visible. The air was warm and balmy, and he could hear the waves gently slapping the sand as the tide crept farther up on the beach. Soon the moon rose from the direction of the mainland. It was nearly full, and its glow was reflected in a wide swath across the water.

As it rose higher and higher it gradually cast a soft glow over the whole beach. Steve put out his fire and sat quietly observing the silvery rays penetrate every nook and corner of the shelter. He felt almost hypnotized by the peace and beauty of the scene.

Suddenly the coyote, which had been dozing at his side, pricked up its ears and sat up. It seemed to be listening intently, and sniffed the air with its keen nose.

"What's the matter, Amigo, old boy?" Steve asked as he patted the tense body.

The coyote paid no attention. It was obviously alerted by some presence unseen by Steve. It took a few steps toward the water and stood emitting its peculiar baying sounds, half-barking and half-howling.

Steve was puzzled. What could have startled the animal? It must be something in the water, he decided, as he felt a tingling down his spine. He got up and stood by the coyote. There was no boat visible in the moonlight. "What could it be?" he asked himself.

While he was straining his eyes, hoping to see a boat come into view, the coyote left him and crept silently down to the water's edge. Steve followed quietly and stood staring intently at the silver-tipped waves.

Then he saw it! A shiny black shape was moving through the water toward shore. As it emerged from the waves and struggled through the surf, Steve saw that it was an enormous sea turtle which must weigh three or four hundred pounds.

The coyote had stopped baying and was making no attempt to intercept the turtle, so Steve grabbed its collar and, pulling the animal, moved backward in the shadow away from the turtle's path. He thought that the turtle was a female and that it must have come ashore to lay its eggs.

On it came, struggling a foot at a time to move its enormous bulk over the sand and leaving a trail not unlike that of a small caterpillar tractor. As it progressed toward the high-tide mark, the effort of dragging its ponderous, ill-equipped body over the friction of the sand caused it to stop frequently and rest. Finally it reached the dry sand well above the tide mark. There it stopped and started to dig the nest where it would deposit the eggs, safe from the encroaching surf.

Steve watched with complete fascination as the turtle first scraped a shallow depression with her fore and hind flippers. Next, using her hind flippers alternately, she scooped out a hole in the depression about eighteen inches deep. Over this she settled her body and began laying the eggs.

Steve was surprised that the coyote showed no signs of wanting to interfere. It sat quietly alert by his side, as the turtle prepared the nest and began to fill it. Soon the reason occurred to him. The animal had doubtless witnessed the procedure many times during its life on the island.

"I'll bet Amigo's waiting for the eggs," he thought. "The turtle itself would be of no use to him encased in its armor of heavy shell."

After a long time, the creature seemed to have finished depositing her eggs. She filled the nest with sand by pushing it in with her hind flippers and scraping it smoothly over the top to obliterate any signs of the nest.

Now it was time to return to the sea. Once more she made the laborious trip across the beach into the surf and was finally swallowed up in the waves.

She had no sooner left the nest than the coyote fretted and whined to be freed. However, Steve held on to its collar until the turtle had disappeared. At last, he let it loose. In a flash the animal had found the nest, dug away the sand with its paws, and was busily devouring eggs.

Steve hobbled to the nest. After inspection, he estimated that there were well over a hundred eggs, enough for many meals both for him and the coyote. He had never tasted a turtle egg, but he had heard that some people enjoyed them.

He picked up an egg and examined it. It was still warm and was white and round, about the same size as a ping-pong ball. The shells were soft and rubbery. He broke one open and emptied the contents in his mouth. The taste was neither exceptional nor disagreeable. The eggs would be a welcome change from his diet of fish, and he decided to boil a few in the morning.

"A boiled turtle egg is not exactly what I would order in a fancy restaurant," he told himself, "but I'm not in any position to be particular about food."

He got his pot and filled it to the brim. The coyote had stopped eating and apparently had satisfied its appetite. It lay licking its paws as it watched Steve gather eggs.

Steve addressed his friend. "Don't worry, fellow, I'm getting some for you too."

He made several trips from the nest to the shelter before he had stored all the eggs. It would have been a good idea to have left some to hatch, but he knew that the coyote would dig them up.

"At least I didn't kill the goose that laid the golden eggs," he thought, and he was surprised that he had had no thought of killing the turtle. The meat would have been most welcome fare, but he had been too fascinated to interfere. He decided that if another came ashore on any of the following nights, he would get it.

Chapter 21

THE SUN WAS HIGH WHEN STEVE OPENED HIS EYES the next morning. At first he was not sure whether the night's adventure had been a dream or whether it had actually happened. The abundant store of turtle eggs, however, was proof enough that he had really witnessed one of nature's mysterious phenomena.

As he recalled the turtle's great struggle to move its heavy body and to breathe on land, he was amazed at nature's foible. The creature was only comfortable in the buoyancy of the water, but instinct to preserve its young drove it on land to lay its eggs.

In a way Steve felt sorry that he had robbed the nest, but he knew that once the turtle had deposited the eggs she would not return to the nest again.

"I'm a sentimental fool," he thought as he put a pot of the eggs on to boil. The eggs had to incubate at least a month before the hatchlings appeared. When they did break through the shell, they had very little chance of getting to the ocean.

165

Birds would pick them up for food, and those that managed to get to the water would be preyed upon by every predacious underwater creature.

"It's a miracle," Steve thought, "that any of them ever manage to grow into adults."

When the eggs had boiled long enough, Steve sat down to eat. He was anticipating enjoying his first hard-boiled eggs in weeks. As he opened the eggs one by one he was surprised and not a little disappointed to find that the whites had not congealed. The yolks had cooked hard, but the whites were still clear and jellylike.

"That's odd," he said. "Now why would the yolks be hard and the whites still soft?"

What Steve soon realized is that the whites of turtle eggs never congeal as do those of other eggs. The eggs were edible anyway, and he knew that they were very nourishing.

When he had finished eating, he walked down to the water's edge to test his ankle. It felt much stronger, and he decided to begin that day to collect material for the raft. Now that he could walk again he began to feel a feverish urge to get away from the island as soon as possible.

The only place where he had seen pieces of driftwood heavy enough for the raft was on the
other side of the island at the base of the cliffs. He dreaded hauling the wood back across the dunes, but it was much better to transport the

separate pieces than to construct the raft on the other beach. He had already made the decision to launch it from the beach nearest to the mainland, and it was only sensible to build it on the spot.

Before leaving for the other beach, Steve wrapped a long piece of gauze from his first-aid kit tightly around his ankle and secured it with adhesive tape. When he had put his shoes on, he stood up to test the ankle again. With the added support it felt almost as good as new.

He gathered together his coil of rope, a bottle of water, and a packet of dried fish. He intended getting more gasoline from the plane tanks, but instead of carrying empty bottles to put it in, he remembered that he could find plenty of containers in the beach debris.

When he was ready to leave, he called the coyote to join him.

At first Steve favored his ankle considerably, but he soon found that he could put all his weight on it with confidence, and he made the trip across the dunes almost as fast as he had before the accident.

As he came within sight of the Cessna, he had a feeling of homesickness. He had not seen it for many days, and it had been his last link with civilization. It looked broken and abandoned on the long lonely beach, as if it were dying a slow death.

When he inspected it closely, he found that blowing sand and the surf were taking a heavy toll. The outside paint was stripped in large areas, and the metal was rusted and corroded from constant exposure to salt air and water. Sand piled against the fuselage, where it had been trapped by the high tides, made it difficult to get the door open.

The cabin interior was a mess. Stuffing and springs protruded from the seats where Steve had ripped away the fabric, the bare metal of the walls was exposed, and the cockpit panel had gaping holes where he had removed some of the instruments. Salt water had seeped in, and sand had sifted through the cracks, so that the total effect was one of complete devastation.

Steve closed the cabin door quickly. He had no desire to linger longer. It still made him feel sad to see the condition of the plane, which he knew was now beyond salvaging.

There was still plenty of gas in the tanks, and he picked up a couple of bottles from the beach and filled them with gas, stoppering them with the cotton and newspaper he had brought for the purpose. He then set them aside for the return trip to camp.

168   Leaving the plane, he made his way along the beach and over the rocks to the bottom of the cliff where the piles of wood had collected. Clam-

bering over the rocks was hard on his weak ankle, but fortunately the tide was low enough so that he could keep away from the spray thrown up by the waves as they dashed against the rocks.

In planning the raft Steve had formed a mental picture of the size and type of wood he would need. He had seen some large logs in the pyramid of wood when he had found the shafts for the travois, and he thought that they would do. His plan was to lash them together with rope and wire to form a floatable platform.

After searching through the closely packed piles of wood, Steve came across the first log which he thought would be adequate. It was approximately twelve inches in diameter and close to ten feet in length, was in good condition, and appeared to be sound. It had probably been lost from some lumber boat and been carried to the island by a current.

With great difficulty he extracted the log from the pile and looked for others which were about the same size. Finally he located four others that appeared to be possibilities. He knew that he could get only one log at a time back to the beach and over the dunes, so he concentrated on the first. Since it was too awkward and heavy to carry, he tied his rope around it and slowly dragged it over the rocks to the sand.

When he reached the sand, he sat down to wipe

his perspiring face. He had no doubt that getting all the logs to the other beach was going to be a long hard job and would take him two or three days.

As he rested he thought over the plan for the raft. He had figured that five logs lashed together would give him the size platform he would need. It would be about five by ten feet. He marked off a space in the wet sand which approximated the size. He sat down in the middle and tried to visualize himself floating on the water confined to the area. He was aware that a bigger raft undoubtedly would be safer, but it would be more unwieldy to launch and to maneuver. It was necessary to have space for a box of food and water, for he had estimated that he could not possibly make the crossing in less than twenty-four hours, and that only if he was lucky. And he had to have some kind of paddle to push the craft along.

With the size of the raft settled in his mind, he got to his feet. "Now," he thought, "I can't waste any more time except to find food to maintain my health while I build the contraption."

Leaving the log at the end of the beach, he climbed over the rocks once more to the tide-pool area. He was hungry for lobster meat and sea lettuce, and the tide was low enough to look for them. From past sad experience he had learned to wrap his hands to protect them from the lobster spines. He had brought along some strips of plane fabric for the purpose, and he wound these around his hands before taking up his post at one of the pools. He was lucky again; he grabbed a pair of lobsters before they could escape and covered them with a bunch of sea lettuce. Then he rolled them in his jacket to take to camp.

When Steve returned to the beach, he grasped the rope and pulled the log along toward the plane. It was much easier pulling it over sand, but he was not looking forward to the long trip across the dunes. Although his ankle had stood up well so far, it was beginning to weaken from the strain he had imposed on it.

He sat down by the plane to rest and to eat some of the dried fish. After a long drink from his water bottle, he decided to leave it in the plane for the next day. That would save him carrying it back and forth.

The afternoon was passing, and as he still had to drag the log back to camp, Steve got up to go. The coyote had been foraging on the beach, and it came running to the plane when Steve started to pick up his things. He gave it some water in a shell, then he picked up his two bottles of gas and the jacket with the lobster catch.

As he picked up the rope attached to the heavy log, Steve found himself wondering if he could ever manage to build a seaworthy raft. And if so, was it foolhardy to attempt the crossing to the mainland? "Well, I won't know unless I try it," he told himself as he and Amigo headed for the other beach.

Chapter 22

EVERY HOUR OF DAYLIGHT DURING THE NEXT FEW days was filled with intensive work for Steve as he assembled the logs and built the raft. He fell asleep each night from complete exhaustion, but he had the satisfaction of seeing the raft take shape.

It was no small task extricating the logs from the stacks and hauling them across the rocks and the dunes. However, his ankle grew stronger, and after the first trip he was able to dispense with the gauze binding.

When he had lined up the five logs together, they were not the same size, but they were near enough. He made grooves and notches along the sides of each log with his knife. These held in place the nylon rope with which he lashed the logs together at both ends and in the middle. The control wire that he had removed from the plane was invaluable in binding the raft together in several places so that it was more compact.

On top of the logs, and covering them, he nailed and wired a kind of deck made of pieces of driftwood. It had taken him a complete day to find a suitable supply of rusty nails in the beach debris, and he found most of them in odd pieces of weather-beaten lumber which had been buried in the sand for years.

The oar was the most difficult problem. Without proper tools it was impossible to shape a piece of wood into anything usable. He finally solved the problem by attaching his shovel to an old boat hook that he had found on the beach. He used several feet of wire to bind the short shovel handle to the long boat-hook handle, and when he finished he had a pretty good oar.

On the morning of his twenty-sixth day on the island Steve was ready to launch the raft for a trial cruise. To facilitate getting it to the water, he had collected small logs and placed them underneath as rollers.

As he stripped off his slacks, he prayed that the raft would float. So far it was his only chance of getting to the mainland. If it sank or was too unsteady in the calm water beyond the breakers, it would never do for the long crossing.

He grabbed his oar and the length of rope attached to the raft and waded into the surf. The raft slipped along fairly easily until he reached the breakers, then it bounced backward and forward and up and down as the waves spilled on it. Although his arm was nearly jerked out of the socket

174

by the pull against the rope, Steve held on with determination.

Once the raft was clear of the waves, it settled down and floated as he hoped it would. He was deeply thankful as he pulled himself aboard and settled in the middle to keep the craft steady. Dipping the long-handled shovel in the water, he started paddling, first from one side and then the other, to try to propel the ungainly craft along parallel to shore.

Suddenly he became aware of a frantic barking above the noise of the breakers. Glancing shoreward, he saw that the coyote was running back and forth at the water's edge showing its disapproval at being left behind.

"Poor old Amigo," Steve thought as he watched the animal's frantic behavior, "he's so used to me that he doesn't want to be left alone."

He soon forgot his friend as he paddled vigorously to keep the raft on a course approximately two hundred yards from shore. He was afraid to get farther out until he had tested it thoroughly. It was best to stay within easy swimming distance of the island in case the raft should swamp and start to sink.

After floating for half an hour, Steve was convinced that the craft was seaworthy. But it was performing under the best of circumstances, for the ocean was quite calm, and it was still possible that the raft might be inadequate in a rough sea. He made up his mind that it was absolutely necessary to choose a fine day and a calm sea for the journey.

His thoughts were interrupted when he felt the craft suddenly surge seaward. In a few seconds it was caught in a current that bore it along at a fast pace. Steve paddled desperately in an effort to turn it back toward shore, but he was helpless against the force of the current. He recognized immediately that he was caught in what was commonly called a riptide.

Fortunately he had some knowledge of the vagaries of rip currents, and he was not unduly alarmed. The rips were a common occurrence along the coast of Southern California, and bathers were occasionally caught in them. Steve knew that he had two alternatives. He could let the raft continue seaward until the rip current dispersed, or he could attempt to turn it at a right angle and get out of the current.

Since he had no idea how far out the rip extended before it dissipated, he started paddling as fast as he could on one side, in an effort to veer the raft off at an angle.

At last he was successful. He was out of the swiftly moving water and floating calmly again on the gentle swells. He found himself much farther from shore than he had intended. It took a concentrated effort to maneuver the craft back to the breakers, where he slid off and let the waves carry it ashore.

When he had pulled it up on the dry sand with his log rollers, he came to the conclusion that although the raft was essentially seaworthy it was difficult to propel with the shovel oar. It would take more strength than he could muster to keep it steady on a course to the peninsula.

He sat down to think over the possibility of a sail of some kind. If it had a sail, the prevailing wind, which blew from the northwest, would eventually carry the raft to shore someplace along the coast.

As he sat going over in his mind the materials he had available for a sail, the coyote came to lie at his feet. It had been overjoyed to see him return to shore, and Steve was touched.

"Poor fellow, you were really upset, weren't you?" he said as he stroked the animal. He knew that when the time came to leave, it was going to be very hard to part from his friend.

He continued thinking about the sail. What could he use? There was the fabric from the interior of the plane, but it was in many pieces and he had no way to stitch them together. A large enough piece of metal might work, but attaching it to the raft posed a difficult problem. His mind went back to the Cessna. What was left that might do?

"I've got it!" he said aloud, with such conviction that the coyote jumped up in alarm.

"Everything is all right, Amigo, old boy," he soothed the animal. "I've just had a good idea, that's all."

He was positive that the idea was feasible. He could make a small sail for the raft from the Cessna's tail assembly. The stabilizer, which extended through the tail, would not be too difficult to remove. Although he would have to figure out a way to attach it to the raft, he was convinced that it was possible.

He jumped to his feet. He was resolved not to waste any time but to get at the job immediately. The sooner the sail was installed, the sooner he could get away from the island. Now that the way was clear, he could hardly wait to get started.

After a hasty meal of dried fish, he set off across the dunes with his toolbox and the travois. He carried extra food and water, for he was uncertain how long the task of removing the stabilizer would take. And too, it had to be hauled across the dunes on the travois.

His spirits were high as he made his way back to the plane. Now that he believed he really had a good chance of getting to the mainland, the thought of a reunion with his family and friends filled him with feverish energy.

Chapter 23

‖‖

STEVE HARDLY SLEPT DURING THE NEXT FORTY-EIGHT hours. His excitement at the thought of returning to civilization seemed to instill in him almost superhuman energy. Although his body was thin from the weeks of scanty diet, his food had been varied enough to provide his system with all he needed. He was in good health, and he drew on all his resources in his haste to complete the raft.

At the end of the second day after the trial cruise Steve was satisfied that he had installed as adequate a sail as possible under the circumstances. He had been able to remove the horizontal stabilizer from the plane's tail in one piece, and it now stood vertically on the deck of the raft.

He surveyed the finished raft with a certain amount of pride. The six-foot metal stabilizer was attached to the center of the deck by the ribs of its framework and by taut wires extending from the top to each corner of the raft. Steve had peeled back the metal at one end of the stabilizer to expose the ribs. These he had extended down through an opening in the deck between two logs.

The ribs were bent back and firmly secured around the logs. To help keep the raft from slipping sideways, he had also attached the plane rudder behind the sail as a makeshift centerboard. It could be lowered between the logs through a slot in the deck to serve as a keel.

To avoid sliding off the raft in heavy swells, Steve had also installed a handhold. This was a piece of rope that he had secured around a log and looped up through two holes in the deck. There was a similar device for lashing down a box containing food and other things he would need. At each end of the deck a deep groove was ready to accommodate the shovel oar that was intended to serve as a makeshift rudder. Using the handle as a tiller, Steve was prepared to steer from either end of the craft.

After carefully examining every part of the odd-looking craft, Steve observed with relief, "I believe it's ready at last. Tomorrow I'll try her out again, and if the sail works, I'll be off to the mainland the following morning; provided of course that the weather is good."

Although he had barely slept for two days and two nights, he lay awake most of the third night. He was too excited to sleep, and thoughts of home occupied his mind. He had no assurance that he would make the mainland in the raft, but the closer he got the better chance he would have of hailing a boat to pick him up.

He was up at dawn scanning the ocean. The tide was high, but the waves were small, and the ocean looked calm. A gentle breeze was blowing, and the conditions seemed ideal for launching the raft and sailing it along the coast of the island.

Since the raft was now equipped with the rigid sail and the centerboard, it was more difficult to launch. By sheer determination and clever maneuvering, Steve managed to pull it through the waves upright. When it reached deeper water, it floated steadily for a moment and then the wind caught the sail, and it started moving. Steve seized the edge and pulled himself aboard before the raft got away. Kneeling on the deck, he let down the centerboard, placed the oar in the groove, and settled down to steer.

It was very confusing at first trying to handle the craft. Since the sail was permanently set, Steve had no control over it, and he had to rely on his crude rudder to turn the craft so that the wind was always pushing against the sail. Fortunately the breeze was gentle, so that he could take his time without fear of being blown too far out to sea.

When he felt that he had gotten the hang of it, he sailed the craft along the south coast of the island within about three hundred feet of the cliffs. The raft moved along fairly well, and after fifteen minutes Steve began to relax his tense muscles.

He turned toward shore to locate his position,

and he was surprised to see the coyote following along on the rim of the cliff. As he sailed along the coast where he had thrown the bottle in the water, the cormorants and ospreys set up a chorus of raucous sounds. They were unused to any disturbance, and several of the birds swooped down and circled the raft, loudly protesting this invasion of their domain.

Steve was amused at their indignation, and he shouted, "Oh, hush up. You'll soon have the island all to yourselves again." And they would too, he thought, for the raft was responding well, and his faith in its navigability and seaworthiness was increasing.

When he neared the south end of the island, he decided that he had gone far enough. To return to the beach he thought that he would have to tack to catch the wind, and it would take him much longer. He studied the piece of cloth that he had placed on top of the sail to judge the wind direction.

Once he had helped sail a small boat in San Diego's Mission Bay, so he had some knowledge of the mechanics of sailing. He knew how to come about when starting on a new tack, but the raft was unwieldy and unlike anything he had ever sailed.

As Steve began to worry about getting the raft back to the beach he suddenly realized that the wind was changing. He glanced at the cloth on top of the sail. It flapped feebly for a moment, then blew tautly in the opposite direction. He saw that he was in luck, for the freakish wind blowing off the cliffs near the end of the island had changed abruptly. It was now pushing the sail so that the raft was headed back toward the beach. Steve grasped the shovel oar and, carrying it, made his way on hands and knees to the other end of the raft.

When he had settled himself once again, he noticed that a dark fin had suddenly appeared on the surface of the water a few yards from the raft.

His hand froze on the tiller, and his body tensed with fear. There was no doubt about what it was. Underneath the fin he could make out the long streamlined shape of a shark! It was cruising along lazily at the same speed as the raft. Steve knew that he was in a most vulnerable spot if the shark should suddenly make for the raft. The impact of its heavy body could lift the flimsy raft and turn it over in a matter of seconds. Once he was in the water, Steve was afraid that the shark would attack him.

He shuddered with horror as he imagined the grisly outcome. "I've got to keep calm," he told himself as he kept his eye on the gray shape beneath the water.

He felt a little safer when he recalled that sharks were often only curious when they followed boats. Unless there was blood in the water which they could smell, they did not usually attack a human.

After a tense thirty minutes, he was alarmed to see that the fin was approaching closer from the rear. Was the shark coming nearer to attack or was it merely curious? Steve had no possible way to increase his speed, and he could only wait helplessly to see what the shark intended. As it came closer to the little craft, he could see its broad blunt snout just below the surface of the water. On the underside of the snout was its wide mouth, filled with serrated teeth.

Steve was terrified, but he was determined to try to defend himself before the creature knocked the raft over, if that was its intention. As the shark came within a yard of the raft's stern, he lifted the long handle of his shovel oar and slammed it as hard as he could on the snout! The shark veered away from the raft immediately. Steve knew that he could not possibly have penetrated the leathery hide, but he had at least surprised the shark with his blow.

He placed the oar back in the groove quickly and continued steering toward the beach. The shark still followed, but it was keeping at a distance.

Steve heaved a great sigh of relief as he drew

near the beach. He could see that the shark was lagging farther and farther behind. He was positive that it would not venture into the shallow water of the breaker zone, and he felt safe for the first time since he saw the fin.

Now he was faced with the task of getting the raft through the breakers again and high and dry on shore. It would have been preferable to anchor it offshore, but he had nothing heavy enough for a mooring, and even if he did, there was the possibility that the raft would break loose and float out to sea or be dashed to pieces on the rocks.

As he approached the beach Steve raised the centerboard and slipped off the raft into the water. He grasped the rope and pulled the craft shoreward. When it caught in the breakers, he let it go. He watched it plunge and bounce as it was carried through the boiling surf. Finally, it was thrust on the wet sand, where it came to rest.

Steve examined it and noted with relief that there seemed to be no appreciable damage. As he pulled it up on the dry sand, he reflected that one more such dash through the breakers could wreck it, but he knew that next time it would not matter. It would have served its purpose in transporting him across the water.

He still felt weak from his encounter with the shark. Now he realized that he might have to contend with sharks on his way to the peninsula, but he had to take the chance and rely on his shovel to fend them off if they came too near.

In a few minutes a bundle of fur flung itself against his legs. The coyote had seen him return to the beach and had raced back to join him. As he petted his friend Steve's heart was heavy. He could hardly bear to think of leaving the animal to its lonely existence on the island, but it would never venture through the waves to the raft, and it would most certainly be frightened to death by the long journey across the water. Steve vowed that he would come back in a boat when he could and rescue his friend.

He spent half the night getting things ready for the early morning start to the mainland. He made a small covered box from parts of crates. Into this he put the dried fish, two bottles of water, some tools, the first-aid kit, the small camp lights, and a bottle of gas. He wrapped his few remaining matches in a piece of plastic to keep them dry and added them to the box. Next he burnished a small piece of metal, which might be useful for signaling in the sun if he saw a boat or a plane. When the supplies were packed in the box, he closed it tightly and wired on pieces of rubber and plastic to keep it dry. Next he lashed it and the oar onto the raft.

To help in keeping a course to the mainland, he planned to use the Cessna's compass. He unrolled it from its plastic cover and examined it. It was in good shape, but he realized that it would be necessary to remove its correcting magnets to get a true magnetic direction. This was simple, and when he had finished, he set the compass aside ready to pack the next morning with his clothes and the remaining plane fabric. His ragged slacks and nylon jacket were hardly enough protection in the open raft, and he intended to wrap the fabric around his body for warmth.

Steve had no idea how long it would take him to sail to the mainland, but if his estimation of the distance was correct, it would take him at least twenty-four hours unless he was lucky enough to be picked up by a boat on the way. If he did make the complete crossing, he could not tell where he would land. It was only prudent to be prepared to walk for a long distance to find human habitation.

The final task which Steve set himself was the careful composition of a letter to be left on the island with his calendar, in case the venture failed. It was a pessimistic thought, but it was entirely possible that he had overestimated his chances and that he might not survive. If this was to be his fate, he wanted to leave some record of his last weeks for his family and Barbara.

The night wore on as he sat by the fire seeking the appropriate words. When he had filled the pages of paper remaining in his clipboard, he rolled them together with his calendar and placed all the papers in one of the empty beach bottles. He wired a piece of rubber over the neck and stood the bottle in a conspicuous place in his shelter.

With this final task completed Steve stretched out for the few remaining hours before daylight.

Chapter 24

|||||||||||||||||||||||||||||||||||||||||||||||||||||||||||||||||||||||||||||||||||||||

TOWARD MORNING STEVE AWAKENED ABRUPTLY from another vivid dream in which he had been fighting desperately to keep from drowning. He dreamed that the raft had swamped in storm-tossed waves and that he was thrown into the water. He sat up and rubbed his eyes. He was still shivering from his imaginary experience, and he hoped that it was not a portent of his fate.

He glanced at the dial of his watch. It was fifteen minutes after five, and although it was not yet light, he knew that it was time to eat breakfast and make final preparations for the journey.

He made his way in the dark to the water's edge. It was too early to determine the exact condition of the sea, but as he listened, the waves had a gentle sound.

A cold morning mist was still falling, and he lighted the fire for warmth and for illumination. He was too excited to eat, but he made himself swallow a few of the remaining turtle eggs. The rest, along with the turtle shells full of water, he left for the coyote.

At the first signs of daylight, he was ready to take off. He had made a bundle of his slacks, jacket, and shoes, and he added them and his sunglasses to the packet containing the compass. He lashed the bundle onto the raft, hoping that the plastic cover would keep the things dry when the raft plunged through the surf.

He shook with cold as he examined the ocean carefully. Clouds covered the mainland, but the intervening water, as far as he could see, seemed to be smooth. There were a few visible whitecaps, but these gave promise of a good wind for sailing.

Now it was time to leave the coyote. It had followed at his heels during all of his preparations, and it seemed to feel instinctively that it was to be abandoned. Steve had to force himself to ignore the pleading and forlorn look in the animal's eyes. He hated having to leave his friend alone, but there was no alternative.

The immediate task of getting the raft safely through the waves faced him, and as he concentrated on the job, he forgot his distress at parting from the coyote. The craft seemed heavier and clumsier, and it lurched from side to side as the falling waves hit its deck. It was all that Steve could do to hang on to the rope, but at last he was treading water beyond the waves, and the raft was steady beside him. He crawled aboard with thankfulness and unlashed the oar. After fitting it in the groove and lowering the centerboard, he tied the oar handle in place.

He was numb with cold when he unwrapped the bundle containing his clothes and a piece of the plane fabric, but he was relieved to see that although the outside of the bundle was wet, the things inside were dry. As he started wrapping the material around his wet body, he turned for a last look at the beach. The coyote was nowhere to be seen.

Steve wondered why it had disappeared so quickly. He scanned the shore, but nothing was moving except the usual shore birds.

Then he saw it. The animal had followed him through the breakers and was swimming in the wake of the raft. Steve was amazed. Although he knew that coyotes could swim, he had thought that Amigo would not tackle the waves.

"Now I'm really in a dilemma," Steve thought. "I can't leave Amigo under these circumstances. He'll get exhausted and have no chance of making it back to the island." Also there was danger of sharks, as he well knew.

He made a quick decision. If the coyote was desperate enough to follow him through the waves, it would probably make the trip on the open raft. He would take a chance. The animal was not 191 heavy enough to unbalance the raft, and it would surely perish if it kept on swimming out to sea.

Steve knew that the coyote would never be able to catch up unless he waited. He untied the rudder and with great effort managed to swing the raft into the wind to slow its progress. In a few minutes Amigo came alongside, thrashing the water with its paws. Steve leaned over carefully and grasping the animal's forelegs pulled it aboard. It was wet and exhausted, but it licked Steve's hand as he rubbed the wet fur with a piece of material.

"Poor Amigo," Steve said comfortingly. "You couldn't stand being left alone again, and I don't blame you."

As soon as the coyote shook out its fur, it lay down on the deck near Steve.

After swinging the raft seaward again and securing the rudder, Steve finished wrapping the cloth around his body. Over the padding he pulled on his ragged slacks and his jacket. When he had wrapped more cloth around his head and put on his sunglasses, he felt sufficiently protected from the hours of exposure ahead.

"I must look like some creature from another planet," he thought. He hoped that he didn't look too grotesque; a simple Mexican fisherman might be suspicious and afraid to help him.

When he finished dressing, he took out the compass and set it in the middle of the deck, where he hoped it would keep fairly dry. Since he knew that the prevailing wind was from the northwest, he set a course of north fifty degrees east, allowing for wind drift. He estimated that this would bring him into the Baja coast somewhere near San Ignacio Lagoon if his guess of the island's position was correct.

As the pocket beach receded, Steve's excitement began to rise again. He was aware of the potential dangers ahead of him, but he had faith that he would surmount them. Every hour on the raft would bring him nearer home, and even if it capsized, he would have a better chance of being picked up by a boat than if he remained on the island indefinitely.

The sea was still covered with mist, but before long the sun penetrated it and shone down on the little raft and its two passengers.

An hour passed without a mishap, and then another. As Steve glanced back toward the island, he reckoned that the wind must have already carried him almost four miles toward his goal.

"If the wind keeps up at this rate," he figured, "we'll be on the coast in another twenty to twenty-two hours." In the meantime he hoped to sight a boat or plane close enough to signal.

The coyote, much to Steve's surprise, was quite relaxed. After some initial nervousness, it had settled down and seemed quite content. As he looked at his friend with affection Steve was happy that the coyote had made the effort to follow him.

There was plenty of food and water aboard for both.

The wind continued to hold, and the raft floated along smoothly. After another hour passed, the mist burned off, and Steve could see for a distance of several miles.

Off toward the cloud-covered peninsula, he saw two distant boats. The sun was in his eyes, and it was difficult to determine how far away they were, but he got out his polished piece of metal and began reflecting the sun's rays toward the boats. He moved it up and down and back and forth, so that if the shiny object was seen there could be no doubt that it was a signal.

When the boats continued on course, Steve knew that his flashing signal had not aroused any curiosity. In spite of this he was not discouraged, for every mile was bringing him closer to the area where there should be other boats.

When he turned to look back at the island again, he discovered that a number of sea lions were following the raft. They were apparently curious, and as they came alongside, the coyote emitted a low growl. Steve was not afraid of the seals, but he was worried that they might be pursued by sharks or killer whales. He looked carefully in every di-

rection, but none of the dreaded fins was in sight.

His hand was beginning to tire from holding the rudder, and his body was stiff from sitting so long in one position. As he got up to change around, the raft tilted slightly, and water washed over the deck. Steve's slacks got wet and so did the coyote, but the raft righted itself and floated steadily again.

"I'll have to watch that the next time," Steve told himself.

The seals had given up their investigation, but as the raft sailed along it was followed by other curious marine animals. At one time it was sailing in the midst of a school of porpoises, who playfully leaped in and out of the water alongside until they found other interests and disappeared. Somewhat later several enormous sea turtles swam along and investigated the shovel end of the rudder. Steve was amused. "I believe they think it's another turtle."

By two o'clock he was hungry and very thirsty, and he knew that Amigo must be also. He fastened the rudder in position and opened the box to get the dried fish and a bottle of water. He had nothing for the coyote to drink out of, so he made a cup with his hand. After feeding himself and the animal, he returned everything to the box. He was somewhat worried, for the sun had gone behind some clouds, and the wind was freshening.

When his watch showed that it was 3 P.M., Steve made an estimate of the distance he had already covered. The raft had been underway since shortly after 7 A.M., and Steve figured that it was about sixteen miles from the island, which was still visible. Since the mainland was screened by haze, it was difficult to determine how near he was to the coast, but he knew that it was at least thirty or thirty-five miles away.

By five o'clock, Steve's worries had increased. The sun had not reappeared, and a mass of dark clouds had formed overhead obscuring the sky. A strong wind was whistling against the metal sail and rattling it incessantly, and the wires which secured the sail were shaking with its force. White caps dotted the surface of the ocean, and the raft was now riding up and down huge swells. Steve realized that the hours ahead during the blackness of the night were to be his hardest.

Darkness fell sooner than he had anticipated, for the black clouds kept out what little daylight remained. He was thankful that the expected storm had not yet appeared, for every storm-free hour brought the raft closer to the coast and increased his chances of making it.

The lack of proper rest and sleep during his last few days on the island was beginning to tell on him. His body ached from fatigue, and he longed to close his eyes and drop off to sleep. Only the penetrating cold and his dogged determination 196 kept him functioning. Once he glimpsed lights from a distant boat, but in the blackness of night he knew that the tiny raft would never be seen.

The next few hours were to be the greatest test of Steve's endurance. The raft was continually awash from the choppy sea, and he and the coyote were cold and wet. The animal had crouched down as close to him as possible for warmth and to keep from sliding off the deck as the raft rode the swells. Steve's hands, one on the tiller and the other grasping the rope handhold, were numb, and his body felt paralyzed.

Finally at five in the morning, when a faint light began to show in the east, he could stand his cramped position no longer. He stood up to stretch his stiff muscles, and as he did so his numb hand lost its grasp of the oar. Before he could retrieve it, the oar had slipped down into the water and was carried away in the choppy sea.

Steve watched it go with despair. Now he could no longer steer and the raft was at the mercy of the wind and waves. He was too tired and too numb to get excited over this new predicament. He merely watched with apathy as the rudderless craft turned this way and that, but he noted with thankfulness that the wind was still pushing it forward.

As the sky became lighter, Steve could see the dark mass of the Baja peninsula ahead. Although he was about an hour from his goal, he was too exhausted to feel much emotion. However, as the coast loomed nearer and nearer, he tried to rouse himself to cope with the problem of landing. He warmed his hands by slapping them together and moved about as much as possible to start the blood flowing again in his tired, numb body.

As daylight increased, the details of the coast began to stand out and Steve felt his excitement mounting at last. He was really going to make it even if he had to swim ashore!

He peered at the coast to try to determine where he was heading. It was now light enough for him to see that the wind was blowing the unguided craft directly toward a broad rocky promontory. Steve was alarmed. He could see spray flying into the air as the waves crashed against the rocks, and he knew that if the raft was thrown against the rocks, he would be at the mercy of the pounding surf.

He must divert the raft somehow before it was carried into this dangerous area. He did not care about losing the raft, but he would never be able to swim ashore in the boiling surf and would be dashed on the rocks himself.

His only chance was to rip up a piece of the deck and use it as a rudder. His fingers fumbled with the box cover, and he lifted it off and grabbed for his hammer. He pulled frantically at a board to loosen it from the deck. At last he tore it free and was able to divert the raft just as the waves threatened to carry it in to the rocky headland.

On one side of the headland, Steve saw a protected cove with a sandy beach. This was his goal. If he could manage to get the raft inside the cove, he would be safe. He was still too far out to try to swim ashore in his exhausted condition.

With the last of his remaining strength, he worked the raft past the rocky point and headed it into the cove. There the wind caught the sail and carried it toward the beach at a fast pace. Before Steve could jump off, a huge breaker overturned the raft, and he and the coyote were thrown into the water.

Steve started to swim, but he was handicapped by the padding and his clothes. At last a wave caught him and carried him ashore. He crawled up on the sand and stretched out exhausted. In a minute a wet and bedraggled coyote had joined him, and both lay inert on the beach recovering from the long ordeal.

After an interval, Steve felt strong enough to open his eyes and look around. The miracle had come to pass! He was on the coast of Baja California once again. It didn't matter where, only that he had made it!

Chapter 25

||||||||||||||||||||||||||||||||||||||||||||||||||||||||||||||||||||||||||||||||

IT WAS A COLD MORNING, AND ALTHOUGH STEVE WAS eager to seek help as soon as possible, he removed his wet clothing and wrung it out. His matches had been lost when the raft overturned, and he had no way to light a fire to dry his clothes. He knew that he would have to start walking immediately to keep warm.

As he stood up to put on his wet clothes again, he saw a column of smoke rising from two huts about half a mile away.

"We're in luck, Amigo," he yelled, "Come on!"

He ran toward the huts as fast as his tired legs would carry him. As he approached he saw that it was a turtle-fisherman's camp. Long strips of turtle meat were drying on racks, and a strong odor pervaded the area.

Several raggedly dressed children chattering excitedly in Spanish came to meet him as he stumbled up to the primitive shacks. Two women appeared as the children called to them, but they quickly drew back into the huts at the sight of the castaway.

Steve knew that it was imperative to make them understand his predicament. Calling to them in his rudimentary Spanish, he tried to explain the situation as best he could, using gestures and pointing back at the beach where he had come from.

The women were shy and afraid, but at last they seemed to comprehend. They gave him a blanket to wrap himself in while his clothes dried, and they brought him tortillas, turtle stew, and coffee. They were curious about the coyote, and they pointed at it questioningly. Steve explained that the animal was tame and was like a dog.

The warmth of the fire and the unaccustomed food and drink relaxed him so completely that he stretched out on the ground and soon dropped off into a sound sleep.

When he awakened, he saw that it was nearly noon. He had been so weary that he had slept soundly for five hours.

He sat up and looked around. Two men had returned with the early catch of turtles, and the families were busy preparing the meat for the drying racks. Steve felt his clothes. They were dry and he slipped them on.

When he stood up, the two Mexican fishermen stopped their work and came to talk with him. Steve managed to convey with a mixture of Spanish and gestures his desire for direction to the nearest settlement. Although the men knew no English, Steve gathered from a crude map one of them drew on the ground that the closest place was a small ranch about fifteen miles inland. There, they told him, he would find an *hombre* with a car who might drive him to the nearest town, the salt company town of Guerrero Negro.

Although his hosts were obviously very poor, they insisted on providing him with a package of tortillas, some cooked beans, and a bottle of water for the journey across the desert. Steve was very grateful; he knew that it would be a long, hot walk to the ranch.

The two families waved good-by and called *Adios* as Steve and the coyote started off across the cactus-strewn desert.

The hot food and the rest had renewed Steve's energy, and he could hardly keep from running. The quicker he reached the ranch, the sooner he could get to the town and make arrangements to get to San Diego. He knew that in Guerrero Negro it would be possible to contact his family and Barbara by radiotelephone, and his thoughts flew ahead to the anticipated joy of talking to them.

The town also had a landing strip, and he could arrange to be picked up by a plane. As he gazed down at his ragged and filthy clothes and felt of his matted hair and beard, he decided he would buy or borrow some clothes and get a shave and haircut in the town while waiting to be picked up. He was almost delirious with excitement as he pictured himself once again back in civilization.

As he trudged along he noticed that the coyote, who had followed at his heels during the first part of the walk, had begun to range over the desert. It flushed lizards and rabbits and chased them for long distances, but it always returned to Steve.

By sundown the odd-looking pair were within sight of the tiny ranch. Steve quickened his pace as he neared it. He had no idea what kind of a welcome he would receive, if any. His disreputable appearance might make him an object of suspicion.

The ranch consisted of a small main house set in a group of tamarisk trees, a few other dilapidated buildings, and a corral enclosed by a cactus hedge. Chickens and a few pigs were rooting in the enclosure, and a nearby burro was braying. An ancient pickup truck stood by the house.

As Steve drew closer several mongrel dogs came out to meet him, barking loudly at the sight of Amigo. The coyote's hackles rose, but it knew better than to get involved with the dogs. It ran off across the desert and remained at a safe distance.

Steve continued on to the house. Children were playing in the yard, and they ran into the house calling to their elders. Soon Steve was surrounded by the curious parents, grandparents, and children, all gesticulating and questioning him in Spanish.

Once again he explained his situation in halting Spanish; where he had come from and his need to get to Guerrero Negro.

Finally the father, who spoke a little English, understood. *"Si, si, comprendo,"* he said, "Yes, I take you to Guerrero Negro, but we must wait for *mañana.* The road, he is bad, and my car, she is old. Much better to go in daytime."

Although he was impatient to get started, Steve knew that the *señor* spoke wisely and that he must spend the night at the ranch.

The family shared their simple supper with him and showed him where to sleep in one of the outlying buildings. Before going to sleep, Steve called and whistled softly to the coyote. He knew that it was somewhere near in the dark, keeping its distance from the dogs.

Soon he heard a low whine, and the animal was at his side. Steve gave it some water and some food that he had saved, but it refused to eat. He assumed that it must have found its own food out on the desert.

Although the animal lay at Steve's side for part of the night, it was alert and nervous. Once Steve awoke to hear a number of coyotes barking in the distance. He saw that Amigo had gone through the open door, and he fell asleep again worrying over his friend's safety.

In the morning the coyote was back at his side. It was licking some wounds, but Steve perceived that none of them was more than a surface scratch. He was relieved to know that although the animal had obviously been in a fight with the other coyotes, it had not been vanquished. Amigo had been able to take care of himself.

"Now," Steve thought, "I shall have to decide whether to take Amigo back to San Diego with me or leave him here to fend for himself."

Even as he thought about it, Steve knew what he must do. Although he hated to part with his island friend, confinement in a city would be cruel to an animal so used to freedom. It was a hard decision, but Steve made it. He must leave Amigo behind to live a free life with those of his own kind.

As he fondled his friend for the last time he had trouble keeping back the tears.

The Mexican was waiting in the pickup, and Steve ran to get in before he could change his mind and take Amigo with him.

Soon they were off in a cloud of dust. The road was primitive and full of ruts, and the old car bounced along at a slow rate. The *señor* had told Steve that the town was fifty miles from the ranch, and before he settled down for the long trip, Steve glanced back for one last look at the coyote.

205

It was running down the road after the car and panting with the effort to keep up.

"No, no, Amigo, go back," Steve called, but the animal kept on following in the cloud of dust.

At last it was tired and lagged behind. It stood watching the car get farther and farther away. Steve turned for a final look. He saw that another coyote had joined his friend. It was a smaller animal and might be a female. The two coyotes stood watching the car as it disappeared down the road.

Steve swallowed a big lump in his throat as he called for the last time, *"Adios,* Amigo."

HARPER TROPHY BOOKS
you will enjoy reading

The Little House Books by *Laura Ingalls Wilder*

Little House in the Big Woods
Little House on the Prairie
Farmer Boy
On the Banks of Plum Creek
By the Shores of Silver Lake
The Long Winter
Little Town on the Prairie
These Happy Golden Years
The First Four Years

Journey from Peppermint Street *by Meindert DeJong*
The Noonday Friends *by Mary Stolz*
Gone and Back *by Nathaniel Benchley*
The Half Sisters *by Natalie Savage Carlson*
A Horse Called Mystery *by Marjorie Reynolds*
The Seventeenth-Street Gang *by Emily Cheney Neville*
Sounder *by William H. Armstrong*
The Wheel on the School *by Meindert DeJong*
The Secret Language *by Ursula Nordstrom*
Hurry Home, Candy *by Meindert DeJong*
Her Majesty, Grace Jones *by Jane Langton*
Katie John *by Mary Calhoun*
Depend on Katie John *by Mary Calhoun*
Honestly, Katie John! *by Mary Calhoun*

HarperCollins*Publishers*
10 East 53rd Street, New York, New York 10022